WITHOUT FALLING

LESLIE DICK

SERPENT'S
TAIL

Parts of this book have appeared in *Bomb*, *Semiotext(e)*, *New Observations: Critical Love*, and *Emergency*.

British Library Cataloguing in Publication Data
Dick, Leslie
    Without Falling.
    I. Title
    813'54[F] PS3554.128

    ISBN 1-85242-005-7
    ISBN 1-85242-107-X Pbk

First published 1987 by
Serpent's Tail Ltd.
27 Montpelier Grove
London NW5

Copyright © 1987 by Leslie Dick

Phototypeset by AKM Associates (UK) Ltd.,
Ajmal House, Hayes Road, Southall, London

Printed in Great Britain by
WBC Print (Bristol) Ltd.

I looked, and had an acute pleasure in looking — a precious,
yet poignant pleasure; pure gold, with a steely point of agony:
a pleasure like what the thirst-perishing man might feel who
knows the well to which he has crept is poisoned, yet stoops
and drinks divine draughts nevertheless.

Charlotte Brontë
Jane Eyre

THE INTERPRETATION OF DREAMS

T R A C Y : Why do you have nightmares? I killed a lot of
people in a dream. I was dreaming — there
were lots of bridges, I could see across a vast
expanse of ocean, with these long bridges
going across to the city on the other side — I
was looking out of a window, it was like a
screen, a bright oblong, I was with Judy and
someone else, another woman — they were
suspension bridges, very long and high and
delicate, (they started out as funiculars, not
bridges — that was a word in the movie last
night), they were like a web, like converging
lines, making this distant perspective — the
distortion of scale was *immense* — and you
know that bit of footage when the bridge
begins to buckle and sway, in a high wind, and
the cars are blown off — ?

D A V I D : Yes.

T R A C Y : It was like that, terrifying, first the towers just
started to sway, back and forth, in the wind,
and the waves became huge, and cars and
people were blown into the water — terrifying.
And we were watching, completely powerless
– there was almost an ethical question, we

1

kept saying, this is appalling, this is unbearable, and I wondered whether it would be better not to see, not to watch all these people dying. And then moving into close up — at this point the bridges became more like ocean liners — people thinking about putting on life jackets, but in a very desultory fashion, as if disbelieving their own danger, and a terrible frustration, not being able to intervene — there was a man with children, and I heard a woman say, *put your diamonds in your pocket, darling*, (as if she would survive, bobbing around in the high seas), and then it was in the city, crossing streets, and nearly being run down by fast cars without lights, night, and going to see — thinking of visiting the bereaved mothers, a sentence — *Yes, Henry is still lost* — implying that he might yet be found. This was terrifying. And there was more, at the beginning of this dream, in a house with women, women who wrote books, Judy, there was a baby, ugh, it was just lying around completely fat and naked, smooth like a white seal, sleeping, just lying on a table, and the mother kept saying, do you think she's warm enough — and she was, like a seal, all that blubber — and there was a pregnant woman, dancing, very happy — all these women who had things I don't have, I had to watch the dance, but there was a wall in between, and I couldn't see, I was going to move my chair (that was from that party, sitting in the corner, I couldn't see round the wall) — I suppose it was something to do with Berkeley, I imagine San Francisco as the city with lots of long bridges . . .

2

DAVID: And who is Henry?

TRACY: I have never met anyone called Henry.

DAVID: So. Who is Henry?

TRACY: I don't know, Henry is in the cinema, in movies people are called Henry.

DAVID: Which movie?

TRACY: I don't know, all movies, any movie. They're always called Henry.

DAVID: You see I think the interesting part with dreams is the place you *stop*, when you can't go on. Who is Henry?

TRACY: I don't know. *Obviously* this dream is all about my first terrors, my earliest fears, it seems so odd to me that you can't swim, because that possibility, the possibility of having to survive in high seas, in the ocean, has *always* been there — my earliest memory is on an ocean liner, going to Turkey, and on one of the ships we took, when I was very small, there was a lifeboat drill, and I suppose I couldn't tell the difference between a practice and really doing it, I thought we were probably going to jump in, lined up in our life jackets ready to plunge into huge grey waves, in the middle of the Atlantic. And the diamonds — I always think of what I'd lose, like in the plane over the sea, the little plane from Key West, I thought about losing my notebook, my treasures, I thought of you not being able to swim, would I be able to save you.

DAVID: It's odd, I had a completely different association, people drowning because they'd filled their pockets up with gold —

TRACY: Yes, that's there too — sinking, diamonds in pockets, a fantasy of rescue, salvage, and sinking because she wouldn't recognise the danger of death —

3

DAVID: But who is Henry?

TRACY: Surely Henry is just the son of the mother, the
bereft, he's the son I don't have. My mother's
son, my sister's son. But hang on, we *know*
who Henry is, he's *lost* — that's what's
important about Henry, the word lost. You
remember, last night, I kept saying, what
would get *lost*, you have to figure out what
you'd *lose*, if you left her, and you said loss
wasn't the issue, because loss was something
that happened *to* you, beyond your control,
and I said, it doesn't matter how rational your
decision is, unconsciously it can be
experienced as terrible loss, devastating, the
loss of this infinitely precious object — and
Henry's *lost*. And in my dream, you see, loss is
a cover for murder. Henry appears to be lost at
sea, but really I've done away with him — it's
my dream. I *want* to kill people, to lose them,
so to speak. The large number of deaths, the
scale of my disaster is another cover —
specific deaths get lost in the shuffle — and
some may yet be saved, and some can be
blamed for not saving themselves, but many
are lost, and it is madness to hope that they
could be found. I *want* her to get lost. I'm
surrounded by all these women with things I
don't have, women with babies and books,
women like her, and my envy and rage are
such that I make a natural disaster, a
cataclysm, and sweep them all into the sea.

DAVID: Yes but all of this is conscious thinking, it's
what you *know* already, and I'm interested in
what you don't know — somewhere in your
mind there must be an association with the
name Henry — who is Henry?

TRACY: ... The first time I got to play a man on stage,
         his name was Henry.

DAVID: O.K.

TRACY: It was Henry Hudson, and I read a book about
         him, and I've always remembered it, he was an
         explorer, it was one of those founding fathers
         plays, I suppose I got to play him because I
         was taller than everyone, anyway I remember
         being very disappointed because the stuff I
         found out about him in this book was so much
         more interesting than this silly play — he
         discovered Hudson's Bay, you know, looking
         for the Northwest Passage, and I think he died
         up there, he was shipwrecked. Anyway the bit
         I was really *struck* by was this book claimed
         that the water was so cold that if you put your
         finger in it, your finger would *drop off* after
         thirty seconds, or a minute and a half, or
         something. Which is castration, obviously. I
         was very struck with this, I mean I pictured
         them in this rowboat, and a man putting his
         finger in the water and it *dropping off*.
         Actually I no longer believe this, I mean I'm
         sure fingers don't *drop off*, maybe, I don't
         know, I would imagine that your finger would
         freeze, and shrivel up, but it wouldn't drop off.

DAVID: So you thought about this finger a lot?

TRACY: Incessantly, I've thought of nothing else for
         twenty-five years! I was thinking about it the
         other day. I think I was already scared of
         lifeboats and being lost at sea, and then the
         idea that the water could be so cold that bits
         of you fell off made a very strong impression.

DAVID: Did you enjoy being Henry?

TRACY: No it wasn't much fun. I didn't feel beautiful
         as Henry Hudson. It wasn't like — later, you

5

see, later I got to play the Prince in Sleeping
Beauty! That was great, that was my first
experience of bringing the house down.

DAVID: How, how did that happen?

TRACY: It was great, it was in this huge auditorium, it
seemed huge, I was little, it's probably quite
small, anyway they'd arranged the chairs so
there was a very long aisle down the middle,
and I had to sit on the very last row, waiting
through the whole play for the moment when I
would appear, and wake her up! And Sleeping
Beauty, she was Sharon Peaslee, blonde, she
went to sleep, and some elves, you know, the
smallest girls in the class, dressed in black
leotards, they came out and arranged cobwebs
around the place, to signify time passing,
maybe that bit was a bit boring, I mean the
whole play was completely absurd, you know,
this is the posh New York girls' school, so
what do we do, put on Sleeping Beauty in
French — all these eight year old girls speaking
lines they didn't understand. Anyway I got to
be the Prince, and I was supposed to be out
hunting, and I had to stride down the aisle,
crying out my hunting cry, O-o-o-ay!, over and
over, and at this point the big girls, in the
audience, started to clap and drum their feet,
and it was like, Yay! the Prince is coming! It
was fantastic. Of course I was furious, I wasn't
allowed to kiss her on the lips, kissing lips was
dirty, right, even *I* knew that was wrong.

DAVID: So where did you kiss her?

TRACY: I could only kiss her hand. But I really liked
the applause, it was tremendous.

DAVID: So why did you stop? Or did you go on
acting . . .

TRACY: Oh you know, going to England, god, that
school, you had to be a card carrying member of
the Dramatic Society, it was all run by teachers,
they actively prevented just a group of us putting
on a *play*. It was disgusting. I did act at university — once. Another transvestite role. This is
getting a little extreme, not to say perverse.

DAVID: So what did you play?

TRACY: I played *Jack the Ripper*!

DAVID: What?

TRACY: Yup, it was hilarious, I mean, I'd gone off to
college with my orange hair and my silver
boots, this monster, and nobody would talk to
me, it was ghastly, so I went home after the
first term, in the Christmas vacation, and I
was completely bored with university,
academia, so I decided I should get involved in
some extra-curricular activities, like theatre,
you know, that's what you're *meant* to do at
university, and I went back, I cut my orange
hair off, I let the roots come through and then
I took some nail scissors and cut all the orange
off, so I had this very very short dark hair,
more monstrous even, — and I went back and
looked for a play to be in, and I heard on the
grapevine that there was an all-woman
production of a play about Jack the Ripper
and I thought, that's for me. So I walked into
this rehearsal, all these women, feminists, and
I said, Hi! I want to play Jack the Ripper. And
of course, they were rather relieved, I mean
they thought I was mad, but they were
pleased, I think, because, you know, it was
early days of the women's movement, and *they*
all wanted to be the *victims*. So that was O.K.
And it's funny, because I never really had to

7

analyse my motives for doing it, it seems rather mysterious to me now, to want so much to be Jack the Ripper as part of a great feminist practice (this was '73, right) — the Women's Theatre Company.

DAVID: I can think of a few reasons, off hand ...

TRACY: Like what, apart from wanting to kill women ...

DAVID: Well, you've used the word monster, monstrous to describe yourself twice in the last couple of minutes ...

TRACY: Yes, I really was, I was completely shocking in this play.

DAVID: So did you get to murder them all?

TRACY: Nope, only one I think — on stage. I cut her throat. Which was very subdued, since Jack the Ripper really mutilated the women he killed. But my great moment was — there were two people playing Jack the Ripper, one was his external side, very upright and Victorian, a doctor (a bit Jekyll and Hyde-ish), that was Alice Buchanan, and *I* got to be his secret inner self, lurking around being creepy and murderous. And there was this one scene, where a woman patient sits entirely still in a straight chair, you know, typique nineteenth century upper middle class neurasthenic, and he's questioning her, very formal, and I'm supposed to represent his evil fantasies, like running my hands over her arms, just barely not touching her, typical theatre stuff, ghastly. So I totally transformed the whole thing by completely sexualizing it, and everyone was knocked out, very shocked. Triumph. It was great, because I just decided to do it, and when you're on stage, no one can stop you, — it was like a theatrical *coup*, *I* knew how to take this

crummy scene and make it really alarming,
just go for the cunt! So you get this really
extraordinary tableau, classic: a woman
dressed as a man making love to this entirely
passive woman in her long white dress, who is
speaking to another woman dressed as a man,
as if none of this is happening. It was a
knockout: shock horror sensation.

DAVID: What intrigues me is you managed to find
another Sleeping Beauty, and your action
made good the wrong done you with the first,
when you weren't allowed to kiss her.

TRACY: Yes, *yes*, I never thought of that.

They Begin To Make Love

TRACY: It's terrible, — I just can't be passive, I can't
take it . . .

DAVID: But why *should* you?

TRACY: Oh only because I'd *like* to be, I want to be.

DAVID: Oh O.K., that's a good reason.

They Eat Breakfast

DAVID: So you were Henry, all the time. And he pulls
it all together, really, the seal, being cold, the
ocean, and all the women with things you
don't have.

TRACY: But Henry Hudson, and his frozen finger,
represents the possibility of castration, right,
as I suppose Jack the Ripper could too, he's
impotent, misogynist, wielding his knife as
substitute — even the Prince is, because he's
so purely masculine, she's so perfectly fem —
because you can't have an awareness of the

9

phallus without an awareness of the possibility of castration, right? Maybe trying to include the Prince and Sleeping Beauty in this scheme of things is a little excessive.

DAVID: What did you have when you were the Prince? — there's the finger, and the knife —

TRACY: As the Prince I had my cry —

DAVID: Your cry —

TRACY: So Henry is me, me as a child, not not-castrated, but not castrated either, and it's me the powerful woman, too powerful, murderous — so he must be lost — repudiated. Henry is her *and* me — which isn't that surprising, since on some level I identify with her.

DAVID: You are both too powerful *and* castrated.

TRACY: Yes, with nothing I am too powerful still.

DAVID: It's like patience, it all comes out —

TRACY: Yes, extremely satisfactory. And the two Sleeping Beauties, I never thought of that.

DAVID: But that was so strange, because just after, a moment later, you were saying: it's terrible, it's terrible, *I can't be Sleeping Beauty*.

TRACY: Oh! Oh!

PARTING

TRACY: It's ridiculous, I can't *stand* anyone knowing more about me than I do.

DAVID: But I don't, I don't know more —

TRACY: Yes you do, you know who Henry is. It's so painful — not being able to be a woman.

DAVID: Yes. But there are pleasures — ?

TRACY: Yes. Yes — *such* pleasures.

KITCHEN SCENES

Four women sitting at a kitchen table. It's a big kitchen, white walls, a late summer night. There is no curtain on the window. The table makes room for elbows, empty plates, cigarettes and bottle of whiskey. Hollow rattle of beer cans, barefoot in this heat, the four women sit together, talking.

It appears that one of them blurts and cries and describes, and the others listen and reply. Tears and hard laughter break her sentences, holding her head in her hands, she gestures to persuade her audience of three. The centre of attention is threatening suicide; they're talking her down. This conversation goes on for hours.

No one is quite sure how serious all this is: a matter of life and death, or a perversely entertaining way to spend an evening. A dynamic of exposure and humiliation held them: the more effectively Tracy described her limitless self-hatred and despair, the more despicable she appeared. Nevertheless, her friends kept up a patient contradiction of Tracy's righteous claims to utter worthlessness. She seemed to be both out of control and profoundly self-conscious; it was like some kind of performance. They were tied up in knots of guilt and quiet panic; the complex response of real concern, disapproval, and an almost physical revulsion paralysed them further. Tracy pushed them to a limit; there was a kind of satisfaction in proving to herself that it's no good, there's

11

nothing anyone can do. She was pleased, horrified.

Eventually, she described a fantasy of complete passivity: the dream hospital, white bed, tight sheets, cool and clean. To lie quite quiet, drowsing, with no demands and no expectations. Defiant, Tracy said, 'That's what I want, that's all I want.'

Kate's voice rang out with complete assurance: 'Well if that's really how you feel then you're dead already, you might as well be dead already.' They were tired, at the end of their patience, their defences. They'd had enough. The last word came from Rose, Tracy's friend: 'Well, why don't you? if you really feel that way, why *don't* you commit suicide?' Terrified, Tracy realised, it's true, it isn't enough, they won't stop you, they won't stop.

All four women were drunk and very tired. Sitting hour after hour, smoking, angles of knees and elbows in shifting diagonals, they made an arbitrary composition: four women at a table.

There were reasons, the usual reasons: Tracy had just, the day before, come out of a clinic, she had just had an abortion. (Later the crisis would be attributed to hormone imbalance.) Rose sat beside her, her sharp face pale and blank; she was sullen, unwilling to take her part in Tracy's play. Rose advocated, and practiced, emotional restraint.

These two, Tracy and Rose, shared the flat; old friends, they had only recently moved in; the new, rather empty kitchen was theirs. The kitchen is large, with white walls, and a very new linoleum floor. It has black and white square tiles. Earlier that evening, Tracy had been painting the kitchen cupboards with black gloss paint. She had an idea, she wanted the kitchen to become wholly black and white. She wore American white painters' trousers and a splattered white T shirt. It was hot, hot and dark as it is so rarely in London.

Kate didn't know Tracy very well. Leaning back, refusing whiskey, she gave an impression of detachment, which only exacerbated Tracy's sense of showing off, her sense of an audience. The fourth woman, Lisa, was Tracy's enemy. Lisa had been the steady girlfriend, actually living with Jim, when Tracy fell in love with him, last year, and Lisa's life had been shattered, apparently, when this other woman, Tracy, seduced him, stole him away. That was how they met. Theatrical, Lisa liked to announce how difficult it was to trust anyone any more. Now Tracy indulged in remorse, complicated by the fact that she'd just broken up with Jim, she'd just given him the sack. Broken hearts all round, all her fault. She was the bad girl, worst girl; emotionally voracious, Tracy rose to the occasion, insisting on drama, insisting on some kind of display.

Lisa examined her rival with passionate attention. There was some pleasure in witnessing this collapse: Tracy's bitterness now almost matched her own. Lisa was present in the guise of solidarity — we who have loved, suffered the same man, can understand each other, find friendship instead of murderous rivalry. This fiction was collusive, maintained by both women in bursts. Now Lisa, all loving concern and honest confrontation, was staying with Tracy while looking for a place to live in London. Rose thought they were crazy.

Two days before, Lisa had sat in the bathroom and talked while Tracy silently lay in the bath, listening to Lisa's comments on the visible physical changes of her pregnancy, discussing this abortion as one might discuss a play, a book. Tracy asked Lisa if *she* would have had Jim's baby. Lisa said yes and no.

The two women were fascinated: a classic case of mirror mirror on the wall, endlessly repeating, am I as pretty, as clever, as successful? They were pulled to each other magnetically, a wish to meet one's match, to measure, compare, compete, merge. Like, unlike: they did like each other. They had a lot in common. As always, the man himself, the mutual (boy)friend, seemed to have become insignificant. The initial structure, where the man betrays both women, is turned around when the women get together, and suddenly he becomes the object of exchange, deprived of power. The 'object' in question, Jim, had, it seemed, literally been unable to choose between them, and had gone on the record as saying (to Kate): 'but they're *both* so pretty, dynamic, intelligent, etc.' — as if some kind of comparative list would resolve his dilemma. So they measured themselves, taking his initial misconceived comparison much further, into a metaphysics of narcissism, a mutual obsession.

The summer before, flashback, in the midst of the initial crisis, falling in love, Tracy had gone to stay with Lisa for a weekend. She wrote her a card, saying they really should have a conversation some time, and received this invitation almost immediately. Tracy felt like it was a challenge, the kind you issue to a rival, inviting them to a duel. Lisa lived in Yorkshire then: Tracy shipwrecked herself far from home, put herself in her rival's hands. She saw it as a gesture of transcendent trust, excessive masochism. Sleeping in the same house, eating breakfast together, a physical intimacy, as well as emotional, was released. It felt very dangerous. The time passed in a sunny haze of gentle commentary, describing how they felt about each other, returning over and over to the shared pain, a circular conversation with no resolution. They went for drives in the countryside and wept. It was almost Victorian, this intermittent mingling of tears, but they both found an ironic perspective impossible to sustain. At breakfast the first morning they managed to laugh: Jim liked to eat the little corners of crust, the remains of pieces of toast, with a wedge of butter and jam on them. Both women had unconsciously left their crusts, as they were both in the habit of breakfasting with him.

Now, a year later, in the black and white kitchen, all this history was implicit in each glance, each comment: their coming together, and splitting apart, the struggle for love.

14

Tracy's drive to confess, that night, was an approximation of love, if love is what allows you to fight and to be held. The performance took over when she found that speaking only increased her sense of isolation, once again the monster, the hyena, as she watched her audience recoil. What she wanted was the thing itself, consummation; having to make do with words, still she pushed herself to a kind of nakedness, sitting at the table with these three women. Driven, she was unable to understand her own wish.

As it got later, and things got worse, all four women were very frightened. (Later Tracy wondered why no one had simply put her to bed — as if an ideal mummy could somehow materialize just because you need her to.) No one put her anywhere; they sat, bludgeoned into silence by her words. She was speaking in voices, possessed, with logic wound tight like a spring, unanswerable, incessant: she couldn't stop talking.

They couldn't take it. Packing it in, they got up, going off to wash their faces and go to bed. See you in the morning. Sleep well. In the bright kitchen, suddenly silent, Tracy went on sitting at the table, arms folded tightly, extremely calm.

Very late, Tracy was alone, wandering through the quiet flat. Kate had gone home; she pictured Lisa and Rose lying prone in their dark rooms, sleepy. Tracy was high on panic, rising and rising. She telephoned Jim, asked him to come over. He was frightened and willing to come. Listening for the doorbell, she went into her room and experimented with an old razor and her wrist. Ineffectual scratches: it was extremely difficult to push hard enough to hurt herself. (The razor, retrieved from the recesses of her sewing box, was a derelict from a summer of cocaine three, four years before. It was quite blunt.)

Eventually Jim showed up, very upset to see her in this state. There was nothing to be said. Tracy had finally talked herself out, complaints, cries, demands all exhausted.

They found themselves crouching, squatting down on the squares of the kitchen floor, at different ends of the room, leaning curved backs against opposite walls, not facing each other. Far away, distant, stuck on the black and white tiles. He said, 'It's like a game of chess.'

Quickly she said, 'No it's not — *look* there's blood.' She stuck the sharp kitchen knife into the back of her hand, spread out on the floor. Sudden, shock, fear, shock, it's nothing, it's something, pain. It looked terrifying: her hand swelled up extremely quickly. Paper towels suffused with blood. Blood on the floor.

Rose was woken up to drive them to the hospital. Severely wounded, Tracy was laughing, vivacious. Efficient, they were almost relieved to have something to do. At the outpatients, she refused to go into the little theatre where they sew wounds up alone, Rose must come too. This was against the rules, but Tracy insistent, the woman said to Rose, 'You promise not to faint?' They put a little green cloth with a slit in it over her hand, like the sheet over the body in an operation. Fascinated, Tracy realised the woman wouldn't be able to stick a needle into her whole hand; the little sheet broke it up, presented a wound rather than somebody's hand. This was interesting, this was something else entirely. She watched, talking to Rose nonstop. Then a man doctor came in, 'How did this happen?', and with the demanding defiance of a child Tracy said, 'I wanted to see how badly I could hurt myself.' Irritated, he said, 'Well now you know.' And she, desperate for a reaction, threatened, coolly, 'Oh this is nothing.' No reply.

Tracy's defiance faded fast. The shame put a stop to it. And her audience evaporated, in disapproval and disarray, feeling even more furious and guilty. For Tracy, her act was embarrassing, the resort to self-inflicted wounds seemed an acute mortification, an unspeakable faux pas. Alarmed, she wanted to hide the bandage, suppress the evidence; she didn't want anyone to know. Later, she saw the scar as a small, compact warning, a monosyllabic thin pale line, it told her not to resort to violence, to avoid that last humiliation. The knife remained, re-incorporated into kitchen life, the one really sharp knife. Her hand was not badly damaged, no tendons or anything. Her suffering had been put on display; it was again quickly hidden.

MOVEMENT

When they arrived, Tracy didn't ask her friends to wait; they drove off in the big car, as she turned, taking in the leafy Victorian street, houses, front gardens, bright sunshine. She was very tired after the drive from London — sitting in the back seat for a little too long, discovering her period, bright red, in the motorway service toilets, huge sigh of relief that she hadn't bled all over her clean white overalls. But menstrual tension, or relief from tension, added to this swollen, tired, stupid feeling. Motorway driving so dull, warm air circulating through the car, smell of plastic seats and cigarettes, sleepy and dull. Nerves, she was nervous, and tired, and bleeding-to-death, and her mixture of terror and excitement made her feel like a passive object, with absolutely nothing to say for herself.

Standing in the quiet street, she looked up at the house. It was Victorian, yellow brick, quite tall and narrow. The rooms would be large, with high ceilings. The front garden had a low wall, messy with flowers and weeds, and, impressively, honeysuckle around the door. It was dry in the sun, dry and dull in the still bright light. It was probably four or five in the afternoon.

Tracy walked up the path and rang the bell. She could hear classical music dimly. She saw the door was unlocked, on the latch, it swayed a little, left open for her maybe; she sensed the cool of the tiled passage inside. No one answered the bell, a second ring, and a shout, so she gently swung the heavy door and with immense determination and trepidation, she walked

17

into the house, calling out 'hello' with a voice that came out quieter than it had intended. It was as if her energy was disappearing inside of her, while some kind of grim necessity, working from outside her body, got her to the empty kitchen at the shadowy back of the house, and returning to the hall, up the stairs, to find a sitting room, following the dim music.

She pushed open the door of the front room, and saw two open windows, yellow sun, dingy beige carpet and battered big old furniture, surrounded by the music quite loud and full, noticed the piano and the empty fireplace, and Lisa, cross-legged on the floor, immobilised by headphones, unseeing. It was a demonstration: the whole house, this picture, announced itself as before her arrival, insisted on showing what it was like without her, so that she could imagine what it would be like with him.

After only a moment Tracy said hello, feeling her hostess to be somewhat at a disadvantage, and Lisa took off the headphones, and with a slightly sullen air of suppressed excitement, the arrival was carried out. Tea, would you like some tea, I didn't hear the bell, what a nice house, long drive, I was listening to the music — dully, like overstuffed dolls, the two women hid their passion.

Lisa was scrutinized, but at least she was on her own ground. Tracy felt adrift, alone — she pictured a solitary balloon let go by mistake and visibly reducing as it floats away — or maybe just the hostage, in the enemy's camp. She remembered that when Lisa had come to *her* house, she'd come with Jim; he had brought her and taken her away; they had come, almost as a couple, to lunch. It was extraordinary: Lisa had wanted to meet Tracy 'properly', this old friend Jim was sleeping with, so they came to lunch. Tracy's hands shook throughout the meal; later she was proud she hadn't been able to pretend. Here, in Yorkshire, there was the same kind of denial, and assertion of normal relations: Tracy had come, a houseguest, for the weekend.

Both Lisa and Tracy were tall, with a tendency to slouch at the shoulders, neck protruding, tortoise. In Tracy's obsessive comparisons, any similarity was striking. They were both dark haired, though Lisa seemed almost Oriental sometimes, with bright eyes and straight dark hair, cut short in a funny slanting fringe, hair like a slightly tilted beret. French, Tracy thought, or Eastern piquante, despite her height, her slouching: perhaps the type was Parisian Chinoise? Lisa walked like a great bird, a sloping flop across a room, her neck forward, shoulders curved, feet flapping slightly at the end of long legs. This was accentuated by flat wooden slippers, clacking. Her clumsiness was magnetic, actively and unconsciously sexy, a kind of everyday, intangible distortion that pushed her hips forward, marking the joints, the armature of her body. Lisa wore jeans and loose, collarless old men's shirts, breasts soft inside, a prospect of pale skin. Her movements were a combination of laziness, the intense languor of suppressed struggle, and the jerky nervousness of a teenager: the slouching shove. Her chin was exquisite, her neck very long and white.

Tracy also wore her hair short, scruffy, and used little makeup, some pinkish lipstick sometimes. She wore workman's overalls, white painter's overalls that you could only get in the States, with a narrowly striped white T shirt and black flat sandals. Typically, the lipstick was by Christian Dior, an obscure colour that had been discontinued, and the ritual of application (using a small mirror kept in her bag) was more important than how it made her look. Tracy seemed larger than Lisa, both larger and softer, and her odd face lacked that pointed clarity, that definition. When she talked, her face surged into expression, her gesticulating hands, moving body, supporting her emphasis, the different meanings. Silent, her face dropped into a sulk, a bored sulk, or a sad sulk. It showed she was much more interested in herself than anything else. Sometimes it seemed to her that she had trouble seeing anything outside, it was all some kind of distorting mirror for her.

Lisa was different. Lisa had *always* wanted to direct theatre; she was serious, ambitious, hardworking; she described herself as naive. In contrast, Tracy felt herself to be outlandish, melodramatic, neurotic: the girl from New York. Dumped at an early age in an English public school, she was always too tall, funny looking, always accused of drawing attention to herself. Turning the tables, Tracy became a defiant show-off — substituting exotic American sophistication, wit about 'broken homes', 'nervous breakdowns', 'necking', for the English whatever-it-was that placed them so securely. She was aided and abetted by her family's money, which allowed for fashion, treats, a quirky hedonism. Tracy happily described her family as 'a classic B movie', especially during the divorce. She flaunted insecurity, extravagance — a slightly desperate attempt to fit in by pulling off not fitting in.

In Tracy's scheme of things, the crucial quality was a sense of irony. Irony slid over Lisa like a shadow, she could feel some presence but knotting her brows, she couldn't catch it. She was perplexed, she tried too hard, and her earnest enthusiasm seemed to Tracy like an innocence out of place. Which makes them sound a bit like the city mouse and the country mouse, or maybe the city rat, sleek and slimy, and the country rat, bumptious and rough. That was Tracy's perception: her cool self-consciousness a measure of sophistication, Lisa's clumsy enthusiasm charmingly adolescent. But the power balance could shift in a moment, Tracy's superficiality meeting Lisa's seriousness, Tracy's sense of superiority crumbling into guilt as she saw how much Lisa was the abandoned victim.

But they were both the abandoned victim, if only for the weekend — that was what they had agreed to have in common. It was a fiction, describing them both as having somehow 'lost' him, whereas in fact they couldn't give him up. Lisa said she was certain that Tracy's money, and 'glamour', were key issues for Jim; Tracy wanted to make out it was all about love, a point of view only she could afford. They spent the summer waiting for the phone to ring, Lisa working in Yorkshire, Tracy pining away in Brighton, while Jim ran away to London, to escape the exigencies of love. Over and over, invisible to each other, all summer long, the two women made the decision to break it off, stop this madness, forget him. And all he had to do was ring either of them up to have them melting with rueful longing. Which he did, of course.

The Turkish Bath was Victorian, a vast municipal institution of exoticized red brick (ornamented with carvings and small eastern-style domes), it combined the fiction of a healthy town (solid, substantial, English) with an idea of pleasure — 'taking the waters' would be amusing, a decorative adventure, an adventure in decoration.

Room after room was lined with patterned tiles, dubious recollections of Persia, the East: turquoise and green glazes, cool white tiles under bare feet, high wrought iron windows allowed the tall open rooms to hold pale light, the concentrated sun outside diffused and reflected through quietly echoing space. The rooms were nearly empty, quiet women relaxing into limpid sunlight, sagging in cotton deck chairs, their toes stretching on cool floor, beads of sweat on the upper lip, hands hanging, still holding the damp magazine. The constant sound of running or splashing water, as figures trailing white (municipal) towels wandered through to the 'hot' room, or the 'very hot' room, a slow movement through space. The arched doorways pointed in Persian style, Victorian pastiche achieved a timelessly appropriate scene, a place for physical pleasure. It was the centre of the Yorkshire spa town, thoughtfully built for the nouveau vacationers, a dead middle class who planted this grotesque delight, the Bath, as if by fluke, in a setting of respectable family homes, and even more solid family hotels.

It was clear that there wasn't very much to do in this town — a town that lacked even a cinema — and so Lisa's suggestion that they take a bath together was met with (polite) enthusiasm. Tracy recognised a challenge (not to be turned down) to undress together. Some residue of hippy values, she disapproved of her discomfort in her naked body; this shyness was something to be hidden, unlike her body. Lisa was keen, and eagerly explained the ritual (Tracy had never before taken a Turkish bath), the process of alternating hot rooms and cool baths, the wet heat and the dry, the massage, and final cup of tea and newspaper lying between sheets at the end.

They walked, Saturday morning, down leafy streets, to the centre of town, the Bath. Undressing nervously, Tracy considered, as her overalls dropped to the floor, her white, flaccid stomach, rough thighs blurred with freckles, her loose breasts — and realised she had never felt so self-conscious climbing into bed with a man. Tracy had seen her rival years before, naked, in a theatre production at the university — it was long before she knew her name, but she remembered being surprised that anyone who looked so dull dressed, could look so stunning undressed. She had thought, what a beautiful body; she'd been taken by surprise.

They sat together, Tracy and Lisa, in the Turkish bath, for hours. Their conversation limited, intermittent, Lisa spoke of her mother's single breast (a recent amputee) and how she had brought her here, to the Bath. 'I think it was important for her,' she said solemnly, 'it was important to be naked here with other women, with me.' A gift to her mother, a gift to me, Tracy thought, some kind of physical intimacy.

It was sheer pleasure: a series of sensations that cumulatively produced a sleepy relaxation, melting the heavy body, delicious drops of sweat running in a narrow stream along the edge of a breast, down the back of a calf. Tracy and Lisa talking, silent, sitting back with face up, they looked at light and space through half-closed eyes — pleasure.

Later, in an over-articulate, passionate burst, they spoke of display, a way to break his hold, his possession of knowledge —

to see each other naked, to know what he knows — as if the shape of breasts, and the trust implied, were weapons against him. This alliance, made of shared vulnerability, was a way to turn the tables, to exclude as he had excluded each of them, to make up another scenario.

Eventually, lying on two parallel marble slabs, they were massaged, each attended by an expert woman, scrubbing, scraping, pummelling their flesh. Lisa and Tracy looked across the gap at each other, close enough to touch if both reached out a hand, as they lay on their stomachs and then their backs, heads supported by a worn wooden block, smiling. The final, blissful, primal pleasure was being washed — lathered with strong white soap on big glove-flannels, lying limp as the big upright woman rubbed and scrubbed the soap all up and down the flat body, and to finish, flings a bucket of cool, clean water over them, water splashing off marble, bodies dripping, shining.

Afterwards, they reclined for the regulation rest, in a dormitory of high narrow beds, varnished wood and heavy sheets, a transition, bringing them out of infant bliss and back to the world, to separation.

The two women stood together, by the window, the mirror, in a too-large bathroom, ex-bedroom, designated as such by the seemingly arbitrary positioning of elements: tub, loo, sink. An expanse of dusty carpet stretched to the other, pale green wall, reached a battered laundry basket, draped sock. Below the mirror a narrow shelf held the small irreducibles of the cosmetic or medicinal sort. Tracy washed her face: a process of splashing warm water over and over. Lisa stood, in her usual propped semi-slouch, leaning against the window frame, watching, and they exchanged intimacies.

But their conversation, being as it was, not between friends, always had an edge, a nervy edge on it: each 'intimacy' was

23

secreted like a bright stone, to add to their meagre store of known facts, to be pored over after, when alone, and once again faced with the question, who is this woman? how is she different to, the same as, me?

Lisa's mastitis: 'It was so bad — my breasts hurt so much — when I went up stairs, I would cry out.' It happened when she came off the pill, 'I had hepatitis you know, when I was doing finals, I was really ill, it's amazing I managed those exams —' 'Not to mention getting a first —' 'But the doctors said I should stop taking the pill . . .' — when Lisa and Jim were first in love, 'He couldn't touch my breasts when we made love' — now she still had an IUD, *and* took the pill (to suppress the mastitis) — no danger of pregnancy at least.

Tracy interjected sympathetic exclamations as she took in the (eroticized) image of Lisa climbing stairs, holding swollen breasts gently as they radiate pain with each small jolt. And matched each story with her own, the Copper 7 that fell out, the clap clinic nightmare, spinning out the repetitions, a simple ritual of women's talk: illness associated with sexuality, allowing the circling round each other, finding out, while making these gestures, telling tales of weakness.

Neither woman put on makeup. Standing in the bathroom together, examining each other, like kids.

That weekend Lisa told Tracy about her year in Paris: her work, her transformation, love, independence. She'd had a serious affair with an older woman, Julie; she'd *changed* she said. Julie was French, an artist, very sophisticated. Tracy, a good listener, made up (erotic) pictures of Lisa and Julie, of a Paris where, as Lisa excitedly said — 'We kissed in the street!' She said, 'The Parisians were shocked, they called us names when we kissed in the street.'

Although Tracy didn't often go to bed with other women, she had a vivid idea, or memory of the wonderful reciprocity of mirror-image anatomy — the same gesture, the same response, — it seemed so free of the discomforts of difference. She knew this fantasy of a possible sexual relation was implicit in her attachment to Lisa. Perhaps it was the only possible resolution to their rivalry, the way to break the mirror-fix, to make sex make pain and pleasure make sense, mixed up, together.

Years later, meeting by chance in other women's kitchens, these two still found it impossible to take their eyes off each other, oblivious to the other people in the room. Like lovers, obsessed, they devoured each other with wide open eyes, tigers glaring, gazing, a dangerous pleasure. As if the other might go for a knife, if one blinked or turned away.

'And there are my ladies,' she said, gesturing to a wall scattered with postcards. Tracy was silent; two years before, she too had made a wall scattered with postcards, the wall facing her desk, and she'd realised, after a while, that they were every single one pictures of women — images unconsciously chosen and slowly put together: no flowers, no landscapes, no groups, just women. She was struck. And here was Lisa, a similar wall, all women — what's the difference? Tracy didn't look closely, fearful of finding too many of the same postcards, and turned to the rest of the room.

A large double bed, with a teddy bear, old and bashed, in a small knitted jacket, propped between the pillows. 'That's Jim's bear,' Lisa said, picking it up. 'He's had it since he was two.' 'Gosh.' 'He left it here, he said —', she made a sound between a snort and a giggle, 'he said he could keep me company.' And the two women wandered out, Tracy covering the transition with some politeness like 'it's a lovely house', which it wasn't particularly, just big (low rent in Yorkshire) and sunny. It seemed like quite a grownup house really, with so many rooms, and a piano, and a front and back garden —

not like the cramped, damp, dark flats of college days. Yet Jim had been something between a wife and a child in this house; avoiding his own ambitions, he was the perfect partner, cultured, intelligent, helpful. Tracy pictured him welcoming Lisa home after a hard day at the theatre, discussing all the different difficult personalities, primadonnas, technicians, her boss. Jim finally getting a job, shop assistant, in a hardware store, while Lisa played the bright young hotshot, directing Poliakoff and Shakespeare with verve and dash. At home (behind the scenes?) she could collapse, and, she said, Jim would reassure her.

'We'd read through plays together, talk through all my ideas, and he gave me so much advice — you know he wrote the programme notes for my production of *A Doll's House* —'

As far as Tracy could tell, their skills and talents complemented and balanced each other — just like Tracy's picture, idealized, of a Marriage. At home, they played duets together, piano and 'cello. They had played duets together. Was it over?

Tracy's remorse coloured this picture; she'd never *intended* to wreak devastation, fall in love. She felt bad, thinking that when Jim was at her place, they would put David Bowie on and go to bed. She felt she couldn't compete — at least not with the 'cello. Frantically searching for an equivalent, Tracy realised that what she had to offer was instability; she could be wilder, more glamorous, less conventional. It was a bit sick-making to acknowledge that her status as wild and dangerous rested on Lisa and Jim's sane domesticity. Tracy found herself at sea, immersed in contradictory pictures, and resorting to guilt: guilt laced with envy, like green veins in grey rock. It was all wrong, this is where he belonged, in this sunny house, theatre people, no question, here, safe, keeping her safe, safe with Lisa.

The seduction was imaginary.

At the party, they danced, it was hot, and she felt his erection against the soft inside of her thigh. In a rush, she went on, and on — more and more, until it was clear to her. Then she propositioned him.

Sitting on the narrow stairs, Tracy said — 'Well, well look, it's perfectly clear that we would like to go to bed together, but you're living with somebody, I mean you're "married", right, so maybe it's not on, which is perfectly all right . . .' He said, 'I don't know.' She got slightly peeved, and figured nothing was going to happen. Feeling rather drunk, she realised she was hungry, and seeing a small posse of men of her acquaintance setting off for the fish and chip shop, she called through the banisters, 'Wait, I'm coming too.'

At which point, Jim said, carefully, 'You can come back to my house and eat stale toast, if you like.' She looked at him, and said, in a mock Mae West intonation, 'Is that an invitation to come back and eat stale toast, or is that an invitation to come back and eat stale toast?' He replied, firmly, 'It's an invitation to come sit in my kitchen and eat stale toast.'

She said, 'O.K.' The decision was definite. This was his refusal.

It wasn't his house (he lived in Yorkshire with Lisa), it was Kate's house where he was staying for a couple of months, while he was doing this work in Brighton, putting on this opera. She walked back with him, in the dark late night, it was just up the hill, around the corner, she was thinking — how much better really to remain just friends — she had known him for a couple of years, she remembered she'd thought that before, with him. This was in fact the third time he had turned her down. She was thinking, how wonderful that he has such a great relationship with this Lisa — how nice that he doesn't want to sleep with me. She'd laid eyes on Lisa once, at the cinema, *Les Yeux sans Visage*, but they'd never spoken. Not going in for them herself, Tracy rather enjoyed getting sentimental about other people's relationships. She liked the idea of sitting up late, in Kate's kitchen, drinking tea and eating toast, with Jim, whom she liked, and fancied, and was not going to go to bed with.

Having disposed of the possibility of sex, she talked a lot, about herself, sitting uncomfortably in the small, dirty kitchen. He listened quite a lot. At three she said, 'I'm awfully tired I think I should call a taxi', and went into the big room to find the phone. He said, 'I don't think you're going home', as he took her in his arms, standing together with the telephone on the floor at their feet. She laughed — 'We're not going to go to bed together now?!' — as she melted with pleasure — as he kissed her neck.

In bed they made love for what seemed like hours and hours. (This is because he didn't come.) When he said I love you she lost her distance. In the morning the phone rang, the phone on the floor, and he crouched beside it and talked to Lisa, while Tracy turned away playing at pretending or trying to be asleep — not present. He spoke as if he were playing at pretending or trying to be alone. He was not. She was uncomfortable.

She prepared herself for the business of Sunday, the morning after: getting herself home, and resting, beginning the process of recovery and disavowal, the fine art of not minding in the least that he couldn't be more to her. She enjoyed this part, it was all part of the discipline, the control.

Later in the day, he came to see her, to, as she thought, re-establish friendship as the dominant mode, to exorcise sex, dangerous spectre, re-assert conversation. But he kissed her, standing by the window as snow fell, gently out of a pale sky. He was going to a tea party; she declined the invitation, tired. He pressed her — 'can I come round later, this evening?' — she found herself passive, 'of course'.

When he came back, they made love, it was about nine in the evening, and they put a record on and fell into bed. The dark windows reflected a huge white room, empty and cluttered, and two naked figures in a big bed. She lit a candle, a cigarette, showed her current books, obsessions, began the gentle self-display, murmuring, that complements the tearing revelation of sex. Yes this is how I am, this, and this. And you? And Lisa?

Paris: night street, just evening, the light changing, a shining black on stones, cobbles, and the wet umbrella shook out — two young women, one taller, one self-contained, laughing into each other's faces, a smile of complicity, a kiss.

A kiss somewhere in extent between the slow erotic and the brisk fond — a kiss that allows their mutual admiration and takes account of, nods to, their desire. It is dark, the white faces stick out, dark eyes searching, the smile and laughter floating, repeating, re-appearing on her face as she recognises, shares the pleasure. They've left the bedroom, they are infinitely pleased with themselves, they are looking to see that the other feels it too, and they are going out to meet friends, to some theatre, to see something. It is time to go, they are going together, and they laugh, and suddenly kiss, and breaking, they head off in the right direction, wanting to touch skin to skin (your glimpsed neck), and simply brushing coat cuffs and fingers — curled, curved, longing. At the street corner, mad traffic oblivious, street lights red and green, their fingers reach, and touch, and their happiness sends sparks — when a woman, old and big, passing, half mutters, half calls out a name, and as suddenly, a man waiting on the kerb with them, strides quickly across, but not before they have heard his disgust. And they look to each other, to see your eyes, bright with emotion, and as the light rain comes once again, they laugh and cross the street, hands held, arms outstretched, as Lisa pulls ahead, we'll be late.

Tracy didn't know where this picture came from.

When Julie came to visit, Jim didn't mind that she and Lisa slept together. Another woman doesn't count.

Looking back on that weekend, Tracy remembered the ruined Abbey, their outing in Lisa's car, and trailing about in bright sun and green grass, with stumps of stone and wall making patterns in the lawn, an arch, a row of steps; attempting an imitation of enthusiasm, but half-hearted: she couldn't quite bring herself to buy the booklet and trace the patterns ('this was the kitchen, this the privy'), and so she wandered through, half looking, until coming to a stop at the tea place, where Lisa had sat down, and tears dropped onto heavy white plates — silent, miserable.

The (long) day wore on, elastic day (long) drawn out by nervous boredom and anxiety, with absolutely nothing to do but talk, the talk circling around and around their pain, until it intersected, and they were talking about him again, making blurred tracks as they went over their rivalry, their loss.

The two women talked about books, they both read a lot. They talked about what Tracy had written in her Shakespeare paper, she'd just finished the exams, and Tracy complained about the university, and Lisa told her about all her brilliant and sensitive teachers, and Tracy bewailed her own. Tracy was continually surprised that they should have so much in common. Lisa was terribly serious, she would ask about something (what did you do your Shakespeare paper on), and they would *talk*. They'd both done English, at the same place, Lisa finished the year before Tracy. But things always came back to Jim — Lisa would say, 'Oh yes, he told me about that, about your poetry exam', and Tracy would lean back, stiffening: this false intimacy, where so much was known vicariously, a love affair (almost) by proxy.

Lisa told her about being so angry with Jim, when he first started sleeping with Tracy, she came down for a weekend in Brighton with him, and became so angry that she'd gone to see an old friend, and lover, Paul, and fucked him, and then driven back to climb into Jim's narrow bed, she said, 'still wet and smelling of sex with Paul'. Tracy was rather shocked, but sympathetic, despite her distaste. Yet when Jim spoke of it to her, hurt and really disgusted, Tracy said, 'She was showing you how she felt, she was showing you what you were doing to her.' He didn't see, wouldn't, and it was hard for Tracy really to identify with Lisa's gesture: it was too dramatic, too literal for her.

That weekend, when Lisa was staying in Brighton with Jim, Tracy was terrified of running into them in the street — it's a small town. She pictured meeting them outside the shopping centre on the high street, a meeting where they would be the couple, and she would be alone, and they would all three be very polite, and say hello, and she, Tracy, would fall down flat, in a faint. Alternatively, she would say hello, and vomit all over their feet. Alternatively, she would say hello, and lie down on the pavement, and die. It never happened.

Other people sighted them, having tea, visiting friends, and Tracy heard, through the grapevine, what they'd been up to. She felt ostracized, partly because she found herself scrupulously sticking to her side of town, avoiding the main thoroughfares where they might collide. When Jim came by to pick up his razor she felt like a discarded mistress, and tried to act the part of detached yet affectionate woman friend, some idea from some French novel, or movie — Simone Signoret? She was getting angry. She was in love. She sat at her table and stared, paralysed, stuck between pain and pleasure.

Later, she was told, by Jonathan, that the streets near Jim's house were covered in graffitti saying JIM LOVES LISA. She laughed at the coincidence: another pair of lovers, Jim and Lisa, in this small town. A day later, she saw a couple of these announcements, and later on a long white wall, in tall letters, and again on the pavement. JIM LOVES LISA. When she saw him again, she told him about it, expecting an ironic laugh — extraordinary, really. But he said, 'Yes, I know, I wrote them.' She was aghast. He said, 'Yes when Lisa came to see me, I knew she was upset, about you, and me and — oh it's so sickening, such a typical empty romantic gesture — so theatrical — I had written this grafitti everywhere, and so I said let's go for a walk, and we walked through the streets and everywhere she looked she saw — I even, you know the bench in the churchyard, I said, let's sit down, and she sat, and of course looked at the ground, and there it was again. Isn't it disgusting?'

Tracy was remembering Jonathan's look of amazement; she couldn't believe it. She was the one who had to live in this town, walk through these streets. Jim loves Lisa. 'No,' she said. 'I think it sounds very poetic, very romantic.'

Throughout that summer, that time, when she would see Jim sometimes, when he was not elsewhere, with Lisa, the idea of Lisa was always present, by no means the least significant element in their relation. The Other Woman, except that was what Tracy was, illicit: jealousy the best, the only aphrodisiac. Her position as adulteress (adultrix?) meant complete insecurity, constant trauma. She believed throughout that she would lose him to Lisa in the end, that he belonged to Lisa by right; she was always anticipating, expecting the sudden transformation scene when he would vanish. For weeks at a time, they would not meet. She was miserable. He would reappear; they'd be inseparable for a while, Lisa off-stage somewhere, out of sight.

Tracy was taken aback when she won in the end, in the autumn, when Lisa came screaming to her — 'How can you want him when he was kissing me in the street outside your house five minutes before he's kissing you!' Lisa left a note for him saying goodbye, and suddenly Jim was hers, handed over, her problem now. She didn't want him anymore, although she didn't know then that the erotic triangle had fuelled their passion — and 'marriage', the monolithic couple, would kill it.

The sunny house, late afternoon, Tracy on the loo, the phone ringing, stopped, pause, and Lisa shouting, 'It's Jim, will you . . .', Tracy, very angry, shouting back rigidly, 'I can't speak to him —', and Lisa, '*I'm* not going to speak to him —'. Tracy fastened her overalls, and emerged to see Lisa leaving the phone, and hurtling downstairs. She picked up the receiver: 'What do you think you're doing?' 'Is it so bad? I was going to come and see you.' '*Who* do you want to speak to?' 'Well —' 'Listen, I've got to go, I'll call you when I get home. Bye.' Pause. 'Oh — O.K., byebye.'

Stunned, like being hit in the chest, whacked, Tracy could hardly believe he was capable of ringing up and not knowing who, which one of them he wanted to speak to. An implied either, or both — did he imagine they would take turns at the telephone? This was deeply shocking. She went downstairs, murmuring 'the bastard the bastard' to herself, amazed, and saw the front door open ahead of her — had Lisa run away? She found her sitting in the front garden, dry grass, rich evening sun, burning warmth, crying, holding herself. Tracy put her arm around her — for a moment there was no division, he had with one gesture violated them both.

'And he's so obviously trying to come between us —' 'He just can't bear being left out —' 'It's so destructive, I just can't believe it —' Bright fragments of pain, and the suppressed fury that becomes hurt tears: they felt a physical vulnerability, weak with rage. When suddenly Lisa rose, and ran into the house — upstairs, and thundering down, knees and feet like marionettes, limbs jangling, she appeared holding Jim's bear — innocent stand-in — and Tracy found her in the kitchen, stabbing its stomach with a long knife — murder.

The gashes were deep and long, jagged, the stabbing straight out of a horror movie, in the cool shadowy kitchen, a domesticity unmoved by this violence. Lisa was out of control. Tracy watched, scared, and after a moment stopped her, reached out to touch the thin white forearm, hacking through the stiff stuffing. Lisa dropped the knife, and taking the bear out the back door, she lifted the lid of the bashed old bin, Tracy followed, thinking no, no, brain working, Lisa raising the mangled corpse to drop it in, Tracy saw a shoebox, and presented it, saying, 'No, here, put it in here', (so the bear wouldn't mix with the potato peel and kitchen garbage, smelly), a kind of coffin. In went the bear, and its stomach stuffing, and the lid on the box, and the bin lid — and Lisa lurched back into the house, crying very hard, shuddering.

So Tracy took the role of nurse or mummy, frightened by the impact of the violence, she knew it must be dealt with, somehow, and brain working, slow motion protest, she realised, no. She wouldn't let her do this. Inside, Lisa crouched on the stairs, gasping. Tracy said to her: 'No, I won't let this happen. Listen, Lisa — I am going to get the bear. We're going to fix him — we're going to sew him up.' Lisa looked up, like a child, mouth closing in agreement: 'I'll go get my sewing box.' Tracy retrieved the bear, and Lisa sat on the stairs and sewed him up, with clumsy, big red stitches up his stomach, so the scar would show. Tracy watched, congratulating herself on her impersonation of a psychiatric nurse. Her intervention seemed to have been the right thing, although it was treating Lisa like a child. She felt she had undone the shock, by undoing the murder, she had brought Lisa back — all the way to the violent gesture and back again, to sitting perched on the stairs, carefully threading a needle, and childishly, clumsily mending the broken bear.

But it didn't take care of Tracy's shock and fear and anger, and her ironic awareness, a sort of semi-hysterical laughter that bubbled inside, didn't really help. Jesus, she thought, stabbing a teddy bear with a carving knife! Jesus. The whole thing was bad theatre — and yet, she was there, she'd shared Lisa's enraged hurt, and the violence was real. They'd both been horrified by the sight of the mangled bear, and they both were relieved when it was salvaged, and mended. They made it better.

Lisa said: 'Here. Take it to him. You'll see him, give it to him. I want you to give it to him.' Tracy refused, still playing psychodrama, taking the role of the one who knows what is the right thing to do, she refused: 'No, I won't do that. Send it to him, but I won't take it to him.'

And the two women went upstairs again, and tried to find what it was they did next.

Lisa had put Tracy in Jim's room, to sleep. Lisa described how he never slept in that room, how she had encouraged him to take it over, a room of his own, but he hadn't wanted to, and now it was empty, and the 'cello, and the pictures sat waiting his return. Tracy looked at it all distantly, a display case of his life with Lisa; she had never seen a room of his before, it was cold. She felt, alone at last, utterly estranged, exhausted, and rigid with an appalled calm — a panic she knew she had to control, being here in Lisa's house, and yet she knew she was completely freaked out, and had to use all her familiar battery of weapons to contain herself. Mainly she resorted to disassociation: objectifying Lisa's violence, she could a) look after it; b) laugh at it; c) analyse it; but she couldn't, wouldn't respond. She lay naked in darkness, wondering about Jim, already turning to him in her mind, for meaning, for solace.

Slipping towards sleep, the door opened and Lisa came in. It was very late. Lisa appeared in the light from the open door, and sat on the edge of the bed. She was wearing a bluish silk kimono, white skin inside, upset. 'Are you asleep.' Tracy barely propped herself up, lying with her head against her crooked arm, heavy on the pillow. Lisa was cold, and trembled, and they did not turn on the light. In the thick shadows they embraced, and a kiss was exchanged, on the neck, the shoulder slipping out of her kimono, a breast moved, a tear, shaking they touched, wondering, where do we go from here?

Tracy didn't think she could handle sex with Lisa. She

wasn't sure that Lisa meant that anyway, she doubted her own possibly wishful thinking. Their antagonism was so real, and so emphatically denied, all the rivalry and hatred, and violence couldn't be hidden, not if they were to make love. The intersection of love and hate provoked tremendous desire, but they both faltered, scared, and like Victorian ladies, they simply exchanged a passionate tear and a kiss, and pulling her kimono around her, Lisa slid out, back upstairs to her own bed, the big bed she shared with Jim. Tracy was left alone, agitated, relieved, locked in some place she couldn't negotiate, stuck in a story she couldn't tell. The darkness imbued with passion, the moment they turned away from the promise of each other, turned away, turned back to Jim. A return of struggle, an evasion of love.

The flat was dark, when they got back from the hospital, very late.

Tracy's hand was thickly bandaged, stiff with pain. She held it separate from her, at arm's length so to speak, gingerly. Rose quickly disappeared off to bed. Tracy and Jim went to bed together, naked, shaking.

When he fucked her, it was like being in hell. Against herself, a gesture against her life, for death, extending the limits of her degradation. In the darkness, she felt him push inside her, her glaring hand held aside, her sore, broken womb once again touched, her thighs wide, flower opened. Tracy lay and sobbed in the darkness, overwhelmed, limp, on her back with her knees drawn up, thinking about — the no sex for two weeks after an abortion because of the risk of (serious) infection, thinking (deeper in the abyss) that they were again fucking with no contraceptives, doing again precisely the terrible thing. Damage: self-inflicted, like scraping her face against sharp rusty metal, she was marking herself, she was making scars. Damage. He fucked her, knife

36

into her darkness, she lay there, black blood, her hand
throbbing, pangs intense within the swelling like sound, or
light, the throes of pain — she lay there, passive, her other
hand gently on his ribs, panting, lost, moved by this into a
place where darkness put the meanings together.

There was no pleasure, only the pleasure of pain, the panic
of going too far, suffering, past the edge. She didn't feel she
would survive this, she was obliterated, bright light of self-
consciousness extinguished, no more guilt. Pure pain in
darkness — what she wanted, death.

Afterwards, the crisis faded quickly, diminishing, as her
friends withdrew, enough already. Tracy shakily resumed
daily life; pushing a cart around the supermarket, she was
soothed by this imitation of another woman, her mother
possibly, efficiently checking things off a shopping list.
Simple tedium: she took a shorthand typing course and got a
job, became a secretary. Jim stuck around, her only comfort;
he would take her to exhibitions, or the National Gallery,
when she was incapable of anything else. So the love affair
continued, four more years, too scared to move. And she went
into analysis, where nothing much happened. Despite five
days a week on the couch, Tracy proved incapable of positive
transference, and spent an awful lot of time saying nothing at
all. She grew her hair out, depression, stayed home, baking
bread every other day. This took up time — years: uneventful,
domestic, exhausted. They went to the movies all the time,
Tracy and Jim, and tended to sleep too much.

Tracy didn't talk about it with anyone, she never gave even
the analyst a blow by blow account. She thought of what she
had done that night as a series of appalling crimes against
herself: against the whole institution of the self, against their
monolithic 'self-confidence', against the rigours of self-
defence, and against her own life. She was shamed by it.

It wasn't until after she left him that she began to wonder about — Jim. He had fucked her, he had made her pregnant, he had fucked her again. It wasn't all her doing, it wasn't only her self-destruction, her madness — what about him? Recognising a congruence in their violence, these two embarrassing kitchen scenes, Tracy thought for the first time, maybe the element of repetition was the absence, the displacement — Lisa stabbed his teddy bear, Tracy stabbed herself — did they both just want to stab Jim? To murder the man who didn't or wouldn't or couldn't love her or me or us or them.

Jim stood outside always, disclaiming responsibility, as if it was — all their doing, all her doing. He was their ideal object, the man they couldn't give up, Lisa wanted him, or Tracy wanted him — he wouldn't want, didn't know, couldn't say. Yet it was Jim who climbed in and out of their beds, who said: I love you, I love you.

Pools of blood on the kitchen floor, wiped up, woman's blood — abortion blood — so much blood. When Tracy dropped a bottle of red nail varnish on the floor, a splash of shiny paint on the black and white tiles, she left it there, to dry. It made a hard puddle of red, permanent, shiny. It remained, for Tracy, another sign, marker for that other, real bloody mess, her bad night — she liked it.

I DON'T REMEMBER

Mrs. Stone, a knife, red gash, children, kitchen, floor. She fell down, she fainted, she lay down on the floor, white, pale blonde hair, red blood, children.

It was Halloween — and, exiles, the Americans in Turkey found it an important holiday. Clearly they felt some ambivalence about depriving their children of the signs of a normal American childhood. A further element was their own sentimentality in relation to such childish rituals. So pumpkins were procured — somehow. No one remembers if they have pumpkins there, the Turks that is, or whether, like the black and orange paper chains and other marks of this particular holiday, they were bought at the PX. Or possibly the necessary signs of Halloween weren't so easy to come by, possibly half the fun (for the idle wives, their days suffused with ennui), half the challenge was improvising, constructing out of the harsh alien landscape a little America, a home from home. Orange and black paper cut in strips and glued by an assembly line of chattering, giggling, intent kids. She was too little for trick or treat, I glimpse an envy of the older sister, allowed to roam the apartment building in a little posse, to threaten and be rewarded, placated. They all dressed up. (Dressing up, having parties and dressing up, was a staple entertainment for both adults and children. There was, my mother says, almost nothing to do.)

There were lots of small children crowded into the kitchen, quite a big kitchen, watching Mrs. Stone cut the face in the pumpkin. She was having a hard time, cutting out the inside, she used a variety of implements, including a very large knife, very sharp. She was on display, she didn't seem to be completely on top of it, able. Mrs. Stone was willowy, she swayed, she was bendy like the flexible trunk of a young tree. She was tall, and thin, with that soft thinness that allows bendiness without sharp angles; in memory she seems almost boneless. But perhaps that's because of what she did, the fluidity of her collapse. In any case, I recall her blonde hair, around her face, and a tall paleness, soft, a thin voice. Other women, mothers all, had a sort of sturdy look — Mrs. Stone, loose, long, round edges, belonged elsewhere. She swayed.

Perhaps ten children, no there were more kids at the party, in the living room, scattering, shouting, and maybe six or seven little ones in the kitchen, watching the knife. She had made two triangles for the eyes, — the pumpkin seemed very big, ungainly, a little beyond her. Attempting the second long crescent slice of the mouth, the knife, long, sharp, shiny, slipped, and gashed — blood — a great line open with blood, crossing her palm. It was her left hand, the cut severed her hand from edge to edge, very deep. Lots of blood. Mrs. Stone swayed, and fell. One moment she was upright, the next she was flat on the floor. We little were looking up at her, to her, our spectacle — suddenly we looked down at her, limp, our victim. She had disappeared, leaving her loose white body and this bleeding gash on a hand.

Something happened, someone came, a man, tall — he re-arranged her, folded a towel and put it under her head, made her wake up. I was surprised when she did reappear, conscious, that she didn't get up. We were horrified by this display of weakness. She went on lying on the kitchen floor, her voice squeaky with fear. By this time, within moments, all the kids had come to see, we crowded the kitchen. The man said, stand back, Mrs. Stone is just feeling a little weak. (The man was my father.) She lay on her back, with her red hand outstretched at her side, pillowed on paper towels, blood on the floor. We stared down at her, subdued, squealing questions, horror, is she asleep, is she O.K.? She vaguely reassured her own two children in a breathy whine.

She swayed, fluid with fear, sick with pain, she swayed and fell. No one knows how they fall — she seemed somehow to simply appear lying on the floor, absent. She swayed, and fell, like a tree. Her white hand gashed, lay flat, an open wound.

Lazy, limp, pale; fluid, boneless, bendy; utterly feminine without the maternal, Mrs. Stone, it appears, was — sexy. Tall, blonde, small bosomed — like Iseult, or Criseyde, she belonged elsewhere. She was unhappy. Her marriage was going wrong. She drank gin and tonic. She avoided touching her children. Pale, long, fluid, — she swayed. Fell, red blood, laid out, lay down, fell loose, lying flat, red gash, children, kitchen floor.

Mrs. Stone was my father's first adultery, the first my mother discovered.

They drank a lot, cocktail parties, this little group of pioneers, corporation executives and their wives, the Americans in Turkey. Mrs. Stone lived downstairs from us, in the strangely modern apartment building, built especially for the Americans in Ankara. They gave cocktail parties.

My mother walked into the kitchen and saw my father and Mrs. Stone locked in a kiss, standing. My mother without hesitation kicked my father in the ass, 'as hard as I could'.

Furious: they were young, they'd been married eight or nine years, they were healthy, well-fed, extremely attractive, with two charming daughters (not quite as charming as could have been expected, given the good looks of both parents, but still, not hideous or stupid). This was marriage: recognisable, real, verifiable. My mother was very pretty, she managed the sturdy maternal look, didn't attempt the waif or the harlot. She tended towards bossiness, big bosomed, she stood straight, confronted. She was not bendy, though her bosom was soft, pillowy. But she knew she was very pretty, and a great personality, and she wasn't expecting to have to deal with serious adultery. Whereas my father was a classic deprived child, poor little rich boy, unable to make sense of his feelings, to feel, he fell at the feet of any woman (it seemed) who would hold the promise of love and not deliver. On-off, he needed that distance. Mommy was the woman who promised him a new mother, warm, soft bosomed, sturdy, to cancel the skinny harpy, his mother in real life. But after a few years, the lure of the woman who does not give, who won't look after — the woman who demands, who takes, who refuses — this old wish re-surfaced, rose again to the surface. A wish for love, mother love.

Mrs. Stone was weak, she was unhappy, she had small breasts, pale blonde hair, fluid spine. She was sexy.

My mother kicked him in the ass, a crude, simple gesture. Uncalculating.

Family anecdotes: stories, scenes that have been recalled so many times, repetition, until no one can quite locate whose memory it is. Put in the collective care of the group, we all (separately) somehow remember it — remember the story at least, not the incident — occasionally after the victim, or the hero, has forgotten. Family anecdotes: there aren't very many about us, the children. Tell me again, Mommy, the five year old pleads, tell me when I was two I, and then I — such pleasure, a history. In my family the anecdotes star the parents. The original scene excluded us — so where does this picture come from? A scene described so many times, from so long ago, the first repetition of the story lost in the past. But I can see it as if I were present.

The father, tall, attractive, a young body present under the clothes, embracing the listless, soft blonde woman — her back gently leaning against the refrigerator. An American style kitchen — curtains flounce against the window, the dishes piling around the sink. It is night. They kiss, a reluctance shimmers through their eagerness like shot silk: the pleasure of ambivalence superseded. Her pale eyes, pale skin, pale lipstick — she sways slightly against him, feathery. They are both slightly drunk. No words.

The door swings open, the mother walks in, catches the embrace. Is it that they don't hear her, or perhaps she is quick, silent. Maybe they are rather drunker than I thought. But this is the scene: the father, static, locked in a kiss, his back to the door — the mother strides angry across the kitchen and kicks him ('as hard as I could'), in the ass. The scene fades: what happened next.

This is not my memory. Where did this picture come from?

When she had scarlet fever, she was driven to the U.S. Army hospital in the car; a corporation car, it was a round heavy station wagon oddly painted pale pink. The father took her. She sat in the front seat, weak with fever, a rug around her knees. She was not allowed to get dressed (too ill), so she travelled in pyjamas, a tartan bathrobe, her slippers. She was probably carried over the mud in the driveway, she felt acutely, intensely ashamed to be out of doors in her night clothes. She was too young, four or five, to appreciate the social codes of illness; later, her state of undress confirms a sense of drama, a sign that she was dangerously ill — at the time, it meant embarrassment only. A Victorian scene, the ill child, limp, pale, silently passionately concerned with undress. Her spirits, very low, rapidly deteriorated when they arrived, to wait, father and daughter, in a room (it seemed) full of children. There must have been some adults, but it was the scrutiny of her peers that caused her most anguish. No one else was wearing pyjamas.

The next sequence is difficult to reconstruct. Was this waiting room also the examination room? That can't be right. Dreamlike, this memory feels like an epidemic, perhaps, lots of people, lots of kids, urgency. Was it simply that there were people in the doctor's office, strangers, other doctors perhaps, and her sense of that audience merged in her mind with the crowds of people waiting outside? The door was left open, people came in and out. Abruptly, she was laid out on a table, her pyjama bottoms pulled down, given a large injection, a shot. Face down, she couldn't see who was in the room, who could see her.

Thus the vertical horizontal dynamic — prone female child pale, upright men in suits, uniform — was further charged with the sense of exposure: her bottom bared to the gaping crowds, including Daddy, a fascinated public. The shot (prick) hurt. It is a scene of penetration, a scene of being seen, in which the child's position is passive, ashamed, excited. Strange men.

She was embarrassed by her tears.

The other memory, the other significant occasion for undress, was also articulated around pyjamas, the bottom exposed, and a kind of scrutiny: it was the repeated, ritual spanking. Highly codified, this mode of punishment was indulged whenever the children had done something parti-cularly unspeakable. She can no longer remember any of the crimes that elicited this response, but she remembers the spankings.

The routine went something like this: crime committed in the daytime, Mommy finds out, becomes very angry, shouts. Some kind of confrontation takes place, or sometimes the crime is so great there is no compromise. Then: go to your room, wait 'til your father gets home. Wait 'til your father hears about this. He isn't going to be very happy. The child waiting, dreadful anticipation, full knowledge, aimless, unable to do anything. Later the mother would open the door to ask how her sense of repentance was coming along — are you sorry now? This was merely sadistic. She would instruct the child to change into night clothes. The pyjamas appear.

At length the father came home (from a hard day at the office) to be instructed to proceed with a beating. One imagines the mother shoving a large martini into his hand, as she provides him with the edited version of the crime, and no option: she has promised the child a spanking, and he must carry it out. He sighs (nothing to do with him), and assumes the executioner's anonymity, putting on the impassive masculinity of paternal retribution.

Meanwhile, solitary, the child has become terrified. The time finally comes when the mother appears and sends her to the father, waiting, in the living room. He sits, huge, on the sofa, a hairbrush in his hand: judgement. The child cringes, as he says the fatal words: 'Pull down your pants!' She begins the gesture, but turning to jelly, can't follow it through, and like a giant, enraged by her inability, the tears that have already melted her face, squashing her eyes, pulling her mouth, the high subdued wail of protest — like a giant, he grabs her around the waist, pulling down her pants as he flings her across his knees, and hits bare ass with hard plastic — or wood? — the back of the hairbrush. One fell swoop, one crude gesture, one clumsy sequence, her struggle lost, surrendered to the sheer scale of his swing. Overwhelmed. The child screams. It seems to go on forever. Like sex, it seems to go on forever.

Finally released, the condition of undress is again spoken: 'Pull up your pyjamas!' And while the child sniffles, her bottom glowing pain, a few words of reprimand (I hope you're ashamed of yourself, and such) end the exchange. Once more sent to her room, all charged fantasies of revenge dispersed by the brute fact of physical superiority, she clutches whatever favourite toy and comforts herself. Sleep.

She imagined revenge: an image, while slung across his lap, being beaten, of somehow managing to reach behind to his bottom, to spank him. A circuit of punishment, an intimacy of shared pain — her fantasy is complete, symmetrical, fulfilled. It is impossible. It makes a counterpoint to the definition of sex these memories evoke: the spanking, like the scene in the clinic, makes sex up, out of — exposed bottom (embarrassment), a sense of an audience (excitement), and violence (humiliation). A crucial element is this fantasy of her active aggression — beating and being beaten — that is met, overcome by his absolute strength. So that she is vanquished. There is also, significantly, the element of physical pain. These are the components of pleasure, fantasy — making up a vocabulary of sexuality. Unspeakable, secret. And eventually an understanding: violence can be pleasure, her own violence, only when she is overcome, when it is a matter of meeting her match. To be both carried away and held (safe) in his strong arms. To be beaten.

On the bed, wrestling — playing? Horsing around, we called it. This was sex. Wrestling with the woman who did our laundry — she was Turkish, and plump, and giggly. We were playing — on the bed. I remember how big her body seemed — big, close, brown. And soft, plump. Her excitement overwhelmed mine: we were laughing, fighting. She was over me, huge, close, soft — a breast appeared, round, close, and drops of milk. She laughed, holding it to me, my face. We were too close, she was too big, too soft, too much warm skin. This was sex.

On the bed, playing. I was horsing around with the woman who did our laundry — wrestling, play fighting, play. She was Turkish, and plump, and giggly. We were laughing, squirming away and then caught again, held close. This was sex. Her excitement overwhelmed mine. She was over me, so big — I was little — I was my size, she was enormous, and soft, and close. I lay on my back, pretending to struggle, she held me, leaning over me. A breast appeared, huge, brown, and drops of milk, fell on my face. She laughed, white teeth, sparking eyes, she held her breast to me. We were too close, she was too big, soft — too much warm skin. This was sex.

The room was light, on the bed we struggled, in play, we were horsing around.

Her large soft breast, swinging towards me — her laughing mouth, bright eyes — behind her, clear white sunlight on a wall.

Patterned cotton, full skirt, plump, soft, brown skin. She laughed, we giggled. We shared no language — apart from laughing, tickling, wrestling. Sex.

I was frightened: a baby suddenly, a tiny child, over-whelmed.

When the tornado came, the windows blew in. Big plate glass windows, they fell; there was glass all over the floor. Mommy made us get into bed — with our clothes on. What I remember is the solitude, left in a bed in a room full of glass. One was supposed to be taking some kind of nap. When I woke up there was glass on the end of the bed, I think I was dreaming.

My mother trying I imagine to make us feel 'secure' by behaving as if this was a perfectly ordinary afternoon nap. Hiding her fear, she denied ours. I remember when she came back to get us, she led us indian file, tiptoeing along a path between patches of broken glass, windows had fallen in on all sides, the pathway down the middle was precarious. But we were wearing shoes, it wasn't really dangerous. Frightening: I never thought the glass could really hurt us. I only barely remember the wind, the wind was white. (That is a memory of Dorothy's tornado, not mine.)

I suppose she thought if she left the children together we would panic, or be naughty. Separated, we would manage. Absolutely forbidden to leave the bed, I had to lie down, under the covers — not allowed to read a book, or play. Like the usual afternoon nap, these rules were familiar, cruel, oppressive. Intensity and boredom. Afterwards my sister claimed there had been glass on her bed. She said, it could have cut through the blanket, cut your leg.

When we left the flat, we descended stairs, broken glass, to the basement, where all the wives and kids had collected. Refugees from the upper storeys, we began to enjoy it. The grownups were excited, irritated, nervy.

When I woke up (I never slept when napping) there was glass on the end of the bed, a patch of broken glass on the bedspread.

I remember.

In bed, in the dark room, she felt bugs creeping all over her body. It was like pins and needles. The bed was hard and narrow, it was full of bugs, crawling all over her body, except the parts that weren't under the sheets, her face, and arms. She didn't dare get out of bed. She didn't dare turn on the light. She curled up, higher and higher, to get away from the bugs. Eventually she found herself curled in a ball, like a rabbit, on the pillow. Everywhere else in the bed was crawling, creeping. She huddled, crouched on her knees, hugging herself, imagining that she would be able to sleep, closing her eyes, concentrating. At some point her father opened the door to see how she was. She was scared he would be angry. Instead he laughed and said, that's a funny way to sleep. He pulled the covers out and held them for her to slip back under. She couldn't say no, she couldn't explain. Silent, she was willing to meet the bugs again, to avoid a confrontation. She could return to her sanctuary, the pillow, after he left her. To her surprise, the bugs had gone — the bed was cool and clear as she slid her legs down into its further reaches. She couldn't understand, couldn't explain what happened. Her father kissed her goodnight. She never spoke of this: four or five years old, so many secrets, so many silences.

It's not that there was no one. No one to call.

It's that there was no cry — silenced. There was no space for complaint, for protest. My sister spoke through her body, spelling out conflict through manifestations, illnesses. I learned to think, to draw pleasure from a sensation of understanding. We both achieved a passivity like shackles, allowing only illness or thinking. Later when I learned to read, reading was like thinking, something between words and images passing lightly, flickering, alive, passing through the mind, a psychic activity. It did not challenge my painfully acquired passivity.

A poetics of the ill child's body, the ill girl child's body, how is it read? ('Difficult, not unhappy.') The difficulty of making sense of these bits, out-takes from a conversation whose totality is lost: the relation of parents and children. We have only these cris de coeur, these signs of disorder and distress, as evidence of a failure in expression, a failure in response. Silences. The child constructed, by her disabilities, as a problem: an ill person, she consumes, irritates, she is both held responsible for all her flaws (a lazy eye), and absolved of all responsibility. She is a victim. And it's impossible almost to measure the extent to which it was the parents' need, their wish, to construct her body, her being, as such a problem. The child as object of identification and projection: Little Diana as stand-in, representative of disability, difficulty. The mother

49

needing illness in others to make her well, to allow her the domestic melodrama, to allow tender loving care (what she called t.l.c.), while clucking irritably, almost annoyed. When I asked her if she thought Diana had been an unhappy child, she said, no — difficult, not unhappy.

My sister's body, veiled, crossed by these varying patterns of illness — they do not all mean the same things. The birth defect, the propensity to rash, the dramatic, bloody sign, the recalcitrant eye — read in the terms of the parents, they were all in a sense her fault. The ill person is not ill but bad, and to be punished. The neurotic does not feel himself to be ill, but bad. My sister's pattern of disability made her ugly, acutely uncomfortable, self-conscious — like an adolescent, except she was seven years old. She locked up into herself, shut up, a connection with others sustained (insofar as it was sustained) via the exchange of symptom and care. The connection with me, her little sister, was made out of fighting, suppressed energy unbound, we fought constantly, consistently, for years. Sadistic, she enjoyed making me do things for her, when we weren't fighting. Making people do things for her was a kind of care, but always tied to manipulation, illness.

She looks, in the photographs, miserable. Gaps in her teeth, a sideways, leering, cringing expression, she looks like she's about to be hit. I look bland, blank, absent. It is possible to remotely glimpse a hope, a distant desire for connection, in the eyes of both these children, but veiled by the ugly self-consciousness of the ill child.

Conditions: when she was about six or seven, my sister's illnesses were never utterly debilitating; they took the form of conditions, that made her almost constantly display disorder, but they did not confine her to a sick bed. She was, to begin with, slightly lame. That is how my mother describes it: Diana's limp. A limp which perhaps only she, and Diana, can see. When my sister was born, so the story goes, her right foot was twisted around the wrong way, and to this day her most comfortable stance is with her right foot turned outward. This is no different really from the slight physical idiosyncracies most people develop — except it is, within the family, a recognised flaw, a birth defect, a limp. She's lame.

Secondly, she was subject to intense attacks of rashes, hives. This was called an allergy, but no one ever found what it was she was allergic to — except possibly strawberries, for there was one day when she 'came out' in a rash after eating rather a lot of them, and thus an informal, arbitrary connection was made, which had the effect of depriving her of something she loved to eat, and didn't prevent the rash. (It was as likely to have been pleasure guilt, as the strawberries, that caused that rash that day.) The rash was extremely uncomfortable, and a complete mystery. It was treated with calamine lotion and the irritated monologue of a mystified mother. My sister received little sympathy for this complaint. Like her limp, it was seen as a complaint, evidence of her contrariness. Her susceptibility to rashes was read as in some sense her fault, as well as her flaw.

Then she was discovered to be 'blind' in one eye. Her left eye was described as 'lazy' (as if it chose not to work), you have a lazy eye, she was told, we must force it to work. So they put a black patch over her 'good' eye, to make the slow one develop. Although she enjoyed being a pirate for a few days, she couldn't see. She learned to hate the patch, which she was made to wear all the time; she would lift it up and peer out from under it whenever there was something to see. It is impossible to say this treatment had any effect whatever, other than psychic trauma, and of course the confirmation of her status as somehow (wilfully) flawed. She still describes herself as blind in one eye, and becomes very anxious about 'losing' the other one, the good one.

At that time, however, the illness that overshadowed all others was the condition that led to her flying back from

Turkey to a Boston clinic, and then living in Boston with the grandparents for some months. The symptom was bloody shit, and the famous clinic found that she was constipated. It was never clear why she was left in America when her parents lived in Turkey — unless it was simply to get rid of this troubled, troublesome child, with her miserable expression, and her expressive conditions.

I asked my mother, our mother, about these illnesses, I said, would you describe Diana as an unhappy child? She said — unhappy, no, but difficult. A difficult child. I gently suggested that from the child's perspective, difficult means unhappy, but there's not much point. My mother cannot acknowledge the rivalry and rage that determine her identification with her first-born, name-sake little girl, big girl. Little Diana, Big Diana, mother daughter, ill.

When we grew up, my sister kept trying to kill herself. She would take an overdose, or cut herself up. My father made her drink mustard and salt water. My mother explained that she was ill, it was a sickness, her depression. Again, her suffering was bodily, my sister silent, speechless: it's all your fault.

She sat in the bathtub and cut her arms. All the razors had been taken away, so Diana used the blade of one of those scalpel knives for paper. She made a lattice, a ladder, thin red stripes, marking her left wrist. Like the gentle wrinkles, those thin lines that they say signify the number of children one will have, or is it marriages? Her red stripes mocking those sweet folds, natural bracelets. She made many thin smiles, red splits, the slice over and over, perhaps twenty times.

She cut her right wrist too, less effectively.

She cut, deeper, the inside, soft fold, that soft white skin, inside the fold of the elbow. She cut short deep cuts, making wounds that gaped, yawned, tiny mouths, when she stretched her arm, a flash of gore, then disappeared, closed, when she folded her arm back again. Two mouths, one for each elbow.

She didn't lose much blood, although the bath was red. It seems she didn't know you have to cut up and down, not across, if you really want to let some blood.

The doctor tried to patch her wounds with strips of adhesive, crosswise, to hold them closed. Stitches exacerbate scarring, it seems. She said, 'Oh I don't mind scars, I'm not vain.' As I tried to gently pinch her wounds closed so he could lay the tape over them, as I overcame my reluctance to see, to touch, she said, 'Oh I don't mind scars, I'm not vain.'

At the hospital, later, I washed her hair — shirts discarded, leaning clumsy under the bathtub tap, I washed her short fine hair, since she couldn't get her bandages wet. I washed her hair, pressing warm water to rinse out the thick soap, simple. I got wet, washing her hair.

I killed my sister. It was in Turkey. In a dream I hit her ('as hard as I could'). I gave her a black eye.

In a dream, our bunk beds, she slid down, against the wall, from the upper bed, with a dark green sweater over her head, her face, she appeared upside down. Upside down, only her head and shoulders appeared, her face covered by a dark green sweater, her arms ineffectual. She frightened me. I hit her in the face with my fist, I hit her over and over again. I gave her a black eye.

For a long time, years, the memory of this nightmare was so vivid I thought it had really happened. It was quite a shift to recognise it as a dream, the memory of a dream. It was so highly charged partly because it was so realistic, so lifelike. It is also one of the few memories that remain from that time, the time in Turkey. There is clearly a connection between the black eye, and my sister's eye patch. It seems (now) to indicate an economy of guilt and rage, her blindness somehow the

53

effect of my rage, my rage silenced in effect by her blindness, her victimization.

I was five when my brother was born. He came home from the hospital wrapped in a blue blanket. I loved him. I had recently mastered the art, the skill of turning a somersault. For what seemed like months, seemed like forever, I had been an object of scorn to my sister and her friends, because I was unable to do a somersault. It was the bane of my existence, terrible. At last I'd managed it, solitary practice had bloomed into a clumsy ease. When my brother was about three weeks old, I decided to teach him, so that he would never have to go through a time of not being able to do a somersault. In the classic fashion, he would vindicate me. He would escape humiliation. He would be supreme, different from me.

I picked him up, in the living room, I picked him up out of whatever baby cage or chair he was strapped into, his crib, his carriage, his basket, I lifted him out, and put him on the carpet, and turned him upside down. It wasn't so very different to playing with a large doll. He didn't seem to mind turning somersaults. I rolled him gently over and over, quietly instructing him. I don't remember him crying. I do remember my mother's scream, she walked into the room and saw me holding him by his legs, standing on his head, a precarious balance. I was spanked, I think, and it was explained to me that babies have a soft place in their skull, that it was very dangerous. I don't think anyone understood how benevolent my intentions were. I had (nearly) killed the baby.

But this can't be true, because my sister wasn't there. The anecdotes don't match: a ghastly patching work to put them together. Her story undoes mine.

This can't be true, because my sister wasn't there. She was in America, with the grandparents, the constipation, the eyepatch, she wasn't there when my brother was born. She saw him for the first time when he was about three months old. She came back to Turkey, awkward, leery, she flew to Paris where my mother met her, and took her to Zurich to visit friends, she came back with her eyepatch, and met the new baby, ensconced. Was it then solely the memory of her scorn that drove me to turn somersaults with the baby?

The family as dark violence under blankets, hidden. Diana and me, wrestling with each other, close up, causing physical pain, indian burns, out of sight. If caught, we were subject to the no less violent response of the grownups, we were in trouble.

We fought all the time. I always lost these fights. Yet I went on, there must have been pleasure in the always already failed attempt to inflict more pain than I suffered. I don't remember how they ended — a climax of pain, a submission, tears? Or just abandoned, the victor was the one who got bored and walked away. Who separated, disengaged herself — like sex I suppose.

Difficult children, later we ironically referred to ourselves as problem children. At seven, and five, I imagine my sister was actively unpleasant, even violent (tantrums), and I was passively unpleasant, absent, distracted. Refusing to respond.

Silence. The child, while waiting for the spanking, planned not to cry, as if that was the locus of failure, the moment of submission, humiliation. She always failed in this intent. Later, as an adolescent, when the mother would shout at her for hours, she perfected the brick wall technique of total non-response, which would of course force her mother to goad her more and more acutely, accurately, until she snapped back, a fight. But like the five year old, she vowed not

55

to respond, as if that was the sign that allowed them their satisfaction.

A split between anger and violence: she maternal angry, he paternal violent. Split punishment, the child refusing to cry, the child crying. I do remember one occasion when my mother beat me; she would slap us, and hit us, but it was rare for her to get the hairbrush and attempt a spanking. She was carried away. What I recall is writhing, struggling down a corridor, trying to evade her grasp, wriggle out of it, as she held my arm, and with the other hand, tried to hit my bottom. We flailed down the corridor, me mostly horizontal, her furious, both of us screaming, although differently. Different intonations: her roar, my wail. She wasn't strong enough to sweep me over her knee, she wasn't big enough to hold me still, me, five years old, in a rage. I was shocked at what happened when anger and violence were put back together: we lost control. Together, we lost control. And in the ensuing struggle, it was not clear who would triumph. Except Mommy could always pull the trump card, and call in the executioner: Daddy.

Such a strange relation, mother daughter, we passed the day together (our relation mediated by servants: the cook, the laundry woman, the cleaning woman, the nanny — and later the governess, the nurse), in a sense we passed the day together, locked in struggle, and then in the evening a man would appear, make some kind of intervention in this relation, some gesture. Spank us, or demand a performance, playing happy families. Part of what was happening, in this system of punishment, was the sabotage of a relation with the father; he was not allowed to be the good guy, in fact he was constructed by this scenario as bad guy, if innocent. It was a question of sharing the responsibility, spreading the bad feeling between them.

But it's hard again to recreate feelings; it's possible to see their positions, in relation to the body, to violence, illness — but to attribute specific emotional states is out of the question. They loved each other, they were involved with each other. They couldn't avoid that.

In the economy of transgression and punishment, the roles shift, unclear. Mommy was the object of the crime (you couldn't call her a victim), Daddy the innocent representative of justice (victim?). They must have had a theory about splitting anger and violence; there was no doubt, she was angry and he was not. He had to work up rage, by the sight of the humiliated, cowardly, cringing child, his own humiliation (beating up a kid) feeding into his anger. From this perspective, the child is also the victim, a small body hit hard, police brutality.

Growing: the child's body is registered within a schema of growth. Too big for this dress, or the dress is too small for you — and the new shoes, constantly growing out of shoes. You'll grow into it. Such a change, a shift of perspective, when you stop growing.

The child's body — eating. Refusing food. Eating enough, too much. The child's body — touched. The no-sex, no-nonsense touch — 'affectionate'. The child's body — unconscious. A body inscribed, invisibly, speaking illness, protest, sexuality.

The child makes demands through the body: a glass of water, a stomach ache. My mother thought band-aids could be invested with symbolic value, a sign of being cared for; she was quick to produce them, a ritual of unpeeling, sticking it on an often nonexistent wound. The ritual bandaging was, however, empty — we all recognised it for what it was: gesture. A caring gesture to substitute for caring, a surrogate, a stand-in, an evasion. A bodily contact, touch — mediated by a band-aid. Absurd.

I was immensely sentimental as a child, as were my parents, somehow feelings were not to be named or articulated, if they were they could not be feelings any more, feelings expressed themselves in clichés, in recognised forms: tears, the warm smile, the sudden tight hug, the kiss goodnight. Emotional life reduced to these worn gestures, so easy to fake, so difficult to know if anyone was feeling anything at all. I sense this now, a mistrust of the tears which periodically spring to my eyes when remembering myself as a child, remembering my parents. I know I am crying for myself above all, but at the same time realise that this little girl is a fantasy, a mawkish vision of suffering childhood, to which pictures of freckly arms and wet bathing suits merely add the necessary touch of realism to carry the burden of sentimentality.

Making up: three levels of articulation, three forms — each constructs the object, calling into question differently, making sense.

First there is memory, with its subheading, its partner, dream. I don't remember.

Then there are words: anecdotes, also known as myth, hearsay. This is a different kind of memory, experience displaced into collective memory, a mythic tradition. Like all myths, anecdote formulates, represents the unspeakable, the unthinkable. It articulates the repressed, making an image that allows its expression without the explosive consequences of conscious understanding. Like myth, repetitive, anecdote both images and does not mean. Like myth, it resists meaning, allowing pleasure without interpretation, allowing representation at the cost of understanding.

These stories are hermetic, incomprehensible, in many cases, unbelievable. They are jokes: one does not understand them, one merely laughs, one gets the joke. To tell them again, to interpret, is to break a taboo so great it seems sacrilegious, an act of violence against the family. And the difficulty of taking these monuments to pieces is enormous: the project of interpretation and analysis so easily becomes mere repetition, the ritual continued. Which is where the third form comes in, where the third form intervenes shall we say.

Third is *making up*: invention, a process of reconstruction, attribution, an attempt to make something of the gaps in memory, the blank opacity of these family anecdotes. What it must have been like, what it must have meant, somehow. What it means.

Trying to remember a little girl, the shapes of rooms, spaces determined by the form, the surface of a small body, breastless, dressed in clothes chosen by adults, unaware. Trying to come to terms with the erotic charge attached to that eight or nine year old American girl, myself, the narcissistic pleasure of remembering, reconstructing knees, ankles, freckly arms, shoes. It is a kind of reversed nymphetism, in which I remember, fantasize the pleasure of climbing onto people's laps, or being lifted up, or simply walking down the street beside the tall man in the grey suit (Daddy); being little. I can picture her, running beside a big swimming pool in my bare feet, a wet bathing suit, hot sun; I can almost transport myself back into that body (this same body), those rooms, lose consciousness of her difference, her size, actually become myself as a child.

The child's body speaks — when the child cannot.

This is another family anecdote: it is my story — I am the victim here, but it speaks a set of relations that concern a silence, a brutality. It is a comedy.

When we left Turkey, my father and I had to travel alone together from Ankara to Rome. We took boats (to Athens?), and a train, and another boat. We travelled for about three days, apparently. (Perhaps it was a train to Athens, and then a boat.) In any case, the story goes, my father forgot to take me to the bathroom, and after a couple of days he remembered. He said, Tracy do you need to go to the bathroom? I said, yes.

Roars of laughter — at what? My father's charming inability to look after a five year old girl? My inability to speak? The object of the joke is supposed to be my ability to 'hold it' for up to three days.

Indicative elements now seem to be — my father's denial of my (feminine) needs: as if his embarrassment, his difficulty with the fact of the 'ladies room' was so overwhelming, he could not admit it to consciousness. (This bears all the marks of an infantile fantasy of mine, a fantasy of my father's innocence, his sexual vulnerability.) Was it an issue of sexual difference, or was it simply that there should have been a servant to look after these things? If this issue of the bathroom was symptomatic of his paternal position, I wonder what else he did, or didn't do with me. I imagine he ignored me, as we sat on boats, trains. I looked out of the window.

The other side is my suffering, my silence. It is a comedy, but the joke is based on torture, the torture so extreme that I cannot now believe that the anecdote is true. I think something like this occurred, but the child *must* surely have found a way to piss before two days had passed. Speaking: I do believe the child would never have spoken. This is the key to my horror, and my curiosity.

Why was it necessary for our bodies to speak for us — my sister's illness, my suffering — why couldn't we talk? I don't believe it is simply that no one heard us — it is that we were

60

shut up. Our lips were sealed. So the story tells my misery, what must have been a nightmare journey, surrounded by strangeness, what must have been suffering. This 'must have been' is also distressing: I can only attribute feelings to this child, this body of mine.

The second version of this story is more visual, it is like a Hitchcock film. On the train, by the window, a young man looking at a newspaper, out the window, dull landscape rolling by. Sitting opposite, a little girl about five, doll in hand, solemnly staring out the window. A woman travelling alone sits with a novel at the other end of the compartment, in a suit, her hat on the empty seat beside her. She is not pretty, but sensible looking, presentable. Perhaps she is a teacher, or a nurse. After some time, she stands and slides open the door of the compartment. Greek men lean against windows, smoking, in the corridor. As she goes out, she turns, saying, 'Would the little girl like to come to the ladies room?' The child is dumb. The young man, flustered, focuses and addresses the child — here is the exchange: 'Tracy do you need to go to the bathroom?' 'Yes.' Reluctantly I slide off the seat, clamber through the narrow corridor with the strange lady and find the smelly, unfamiliar railway toilet. Piss. My father meanwhile laughing at himself, realising he had forgotten, he had neglected to, he had omitted a crucial aspect of his role, his performance as — parent, custodian. Looking after.

History: recently I heard another version of this story, doubtless closer to the truth, since it was my mother who told it. Daddy and I flew from Ankara to Rome. When Mommy met us at the airport, she asked me if I wanted to go to the bathroom. 'Yes,' I said. So much for paternal inadequacy and silent suffering. What were the elements that made up the story I remembered? (Of course I *remember* nothing.) Where did this anecdote come from — my wish to excavate scenarios of silent pain?

Can I still salvage a torture scene — how long was the flight from Ankara to Rome, in 1960, how distressing was it? Already my mind begins to deny the new version, to think: we probably flew from Athens, it was the travelling between Ankara and Athens . . . I didn't make this story up. Did I?

Teasing is a form of accusation. And, jokes and their relation to . . ., it is a way of speaking what cannot be spoken. As a teenager, she passively refused to do any kind of house work. She managed this (unconsciously) by proving herself incapable of it, by systematically dropping plates, throwing bowls of sugar across the room, etc. She was going through a phase of being extremely clumsy, she knocked into things all the time. This was called growing pains, she was covered in bruises. But it had its secondary gains, clearly, it allowed her escape — from the tightening tensions of the kitchen with the mother in it, from an arena of rivalry with her sister (who did do it, even cooking), from the feminine position. All of this was paid for, in a sense, by being teased about it. It even resulted in a nickname, the spastic. She was requested over and over again to tell the joke about the spastic and the ice cream cone, the implication was that she was so good at this joke, it was so funny when she told it, because of the element of similarity, identity. Her inability combined with her refusal, her evasion was an endless source of fun. She was teased.

She was teased for not saying, I need to go to the bathroom. Daddy was teased for not asking me. All the unspeakables transform into teasing accusations, screamingly funny. When they finally took her tonsils and adenoids out, and her sister told her she looked unbelievably stupid with her mouth open all the time, she learned to breathe through her nose. But for years they would say, 'Waiting for a fly?', and her jaw would snap shut.

In Turkey, the bunk beds were sometimes dismantled, and placed like twin beds, side by side. Sometimes, together, double decker, they went against the wall. Sometimes it was my room (when my sister was away). Sometimes we shared it, and fought. I got the bottom bunk, needless to say. I like to lay my clothes out on the bed, ready to put on in the morning; I especially enjoyed laying them out in formation, as if I were inside them, and I imagined being able to leap into them, in one bound. Getting dressed was dull and surprisingly difficult, time consuming. We had lots of buttons, it was before the days of easy kids clothes.

I had a toy that was a pillow, hard, in the form of a clown's head, round and flat, with a pointed triangular hat. There was a musical box inside it, and you wound it up at the back, a little gold key folded out, turned. I went to sleep hugging this clown, hanging on to him, listening to the classic lullaby (Brahms?) he played. The hat was green with a yellow pompon on the end, which I chewed. One morning it was gone, and I believed I must have swallowed it.

I am told I never sucked my thumb, not even as an infant. I suspect I was too passive, even for that simple gratification. I never cried as a baby. I played possum, played dead. I remember pretending to suck my thumb after my brother was born; I hoped I would look younger, more babyish. I hoped I would be taken for a three year old, not a five year old. (Taken by strangers, I should add; I only did this in public.)

My mother gave birth to her son in the American military hospital in Ankara. They gave her a general anaesthetic, knocked her out for hours, she woke up and he was there, in a blue blanket, to signify her success. When they came home from the hospital, Mommy looked different. The baby was small, wrapped in pale blue. Mommy gave him to me, she said here's your baby. She must have had some theory about infantile envy.

The story goes that when I was born my mother gave Diana, aged two and a half, a very large doll, and since I was such a placid baby, and my sister didn't see me too often, she didn't realise there was a difference between the two babies for some time. This is another anecdote I fail to believe.

The mother always felt uncomfortable with her sex; perhaps it was because it always had to be for others, and any gesture for herself was in some sense obscene; or because her father and brother, warriors, shouters, called her tart, slut, whore — shouted the accusation of pleasure in front of the man bringing her home at five minutes past twelve, her terrified of losing the boyfriend (either he will believe my father and be frightened off me, me depraved and greedy, or he will laugh at prude me, child of mad Victorian parents, and decide it's not worth the effort, trying to find or force or elicit pleasure in me), or because her attractiveness (beauty too literary a concept in the East Coast debutante meat market), my mother's big breasts, soft bullets in sweaters (conveniently born, unlike me, to coincide with a fashion that happened to match her attributes), my mother's body was seen as her highest card in the gamble for a rich goodlooking wasp husband who ideally would also be kind considerate hard-working and have the makings of a good father.

How to appropriate your own beauty, intelligence, pleasure, when everything around you insists on defining those things as elements in the impending exchange? You get my breasts that other men will desire but only you will touch, my mind which will be attuned to amusing and understanding you above all, and will draw more interesting attractive people to your house, the house where I will live with you, which I will make nice and attractive and intelligent like me, and you can have my children, which I can almost guarantee I will make nice and attractive and intelligent, and you can have all this, all my possibilities, my making, my pleasure, all this for — money, and some tenderness, and your presence when it really counts, like at our dinner parties. All this, I will give you myself, and in exchange, I get the privilege of never becoming myself, never having to sell my work, having already sold myself, I will never have to think about anything really serious again, that is, anything impersonal, I will have the privilege of living without doubt, of winning the respect of my parents, of secure expectations based on the completeness, the extreme comprehensiveness of the exchange. How can I suspect you may not honour our contract, when your side is so easy, your contribution so simple by comparison to mine, which is my whole life; not one pound of flesh, but 125 pounds of flesh blood soul smile me, and the three, no four babies I make for you, it is all for you, you can't possibly not want it.

One time the mother stormed in and found her in a satin slip, the spaghetti straps knotted behind her neck, pulling up the neckline which otherwise exposed her childish chest, a pale pink, soft satin treasure — so clearly meant for a woman's body, becoming a princess gown on her skinny eight year old form, the mother enraged — some transgression the child couldn't understand, some fear or threat. (It had been stolen or borrowed from the dressing up box.) Possibly the issue at stake was childish a-sexuality: she should be in her PJs, cotton, practical, not swanning around her bedroom like a thirties movie star. Possibly she was already angry about something else and exploded in the child's room. This was not untypical. What it produced was simple: a punishment for sexual pleasure, sensual pleasure. A forbidden beauty, narcissism, another secret.

The other one is a screen memory. In New York, the doorbell rang, there was no one there. Night, and a flickering thing, a pumpkin, with its wild face cut out, orange light inside, alight. It was magic, unquestionable: the appearance of the little pumpkin was beyond curiosity, pure gift. But my mother cried, when I called her, to come and see, she was upset. 'Don't you understand? Your father must have left it, *Daddy* must have left it for us.' Crying.

I'd forgotten about him.

He was living somewhere else, he was with someone else, another woman. My mother told me about it, gave me instructions: if he ever took me to meet a tall lady, a tall lady with blonde hair, I was to throw myself on the floor, scream and yell my refusal. I was to simulate a tantrum, in the elevator, on the doorstep, I was to scream. I remember trying to picture this scene (the elevator, the door of her apartment), and wondering if I'd be able to do it. Were the occasion to arise. It didn't. It never happened. He was back in time for Christmas.

Passive action: she says she moved because she had to, his job. Neither in pursuit, nor fugitive, she merely repeated. She can tell you almost nothing about the geography or history or politics of the countries she lived in: that was his department. Her task was to reconstruct, over and over, the American house, the American children, the American cocktail party — under adverse conditions. London 1967, Ankara 1959, The Hague 1953, her social circle consisted of the other Americans, like them. She describes the satisfactions of expatriatism as being 'a big fish in a small puddle'. ('In Turkey there aren't five thousand of you — people like you, there are maybe three hundred.') Being seen to be glamorous and interesting by their acquaintance in New York, she enjoyed being praised, admired for her daring, her ability to prevail — even in a clapboard house in Casper, Wyoming, smelling of the oil refinery, stained with red dust. She says she imagined that her children would become 'international': 'They would speak about five languages, they wouldn't be thrown if things were done in a different manner, they wouldn't freak out at a foreign word on a menu.' She became very good at cobbling together expressions out of her smattering of French and Italian, and excelled at the enthusiastic mime that makes requests. Her husband spoke no foreign languages (he spoke the language of the oil company), he watched her willingness to appear foolish with embarrassment, gratitude. (We turned out to speak no foreign languages whatsoever.) While she takes no responsibility for these changes, these twenty-five houses she has lived in, twenty-nine moves she has made, she did once refuse to go live in Saskatchewan, in 1956, evidence of some power to choose.

The site of the move itself is not the country, the landscape, architecture, or her state of mind, but the innumerable objects, possessions, 'belongings' that come and go, that move. Her emotional priority is to sustain a continuity of things in the discontinuity of place. The same furniture, the same layout — the same bed, a bedroom repeated — no difference, for difference in this movement signifies loss. To move a whole house is to handle, to possess, pack, store, discard, keep. Her moving practice reaffirms her (self)possession. It is a chance to clear out: 'It's a relief, you always get rid of some of the less important things.'

Her classic, epic move was to Turkey, for two years, in 1958; she was given the list by the corporation, and shopped for six months to accumulate the necessary gear. 'We just bought everything, from safety pins to band-aids to hairspray to shoelaces — two years' supply of powdered milk, tabasco sauce for bloody marys . . .', a stove, refrigerator, television, piano — when she told a friend who had lived there that she was taking a toilet seat, he said take a toilet. She did, and beds, furniture, kleenex, clothes for the children to grow into, a nanny, two girl children under five, trailing dolls, dolls clothes, paper dolls, crayons, colouring books, endlessly. She took Christmas presents, thinking ahead. A complete American world transposed. All this stuff installed in a white sub-international style apartment block (post-war, unfinished) on a brown, scrubby hill outside Ankara, surrounded by muddy, dusty fields, and abject poverty, large families living in mud huts, doing without, underprivileged. While the Americans in their concrete tower lived out nuclear family life — as if, removed from its context, displaced, the system of the American family becomes elementary, standing out in grotesque kodachrome, Mommy Daddy and the kids, outlined against the dusty background, the family snap.

Her parents lived in the same house for forty-seven years, and it is this house that she names, unthinking, home. In a sense, the American house she reconstitutes in different places is an approximation of that paternal house: comfy, old-fashioned furniture, with an elegant aspect, a class display.

In her houses, dissatisfaction, the unhappy compromise, is built in. No place is quite right, no shift without disappointment: partly because the shift is what is felt, dismantling, reconstructing. It is the transaction that resonates, while the place itself, difference, is only recognised when the decision comes once again to move. She is inattentive to anything that cannot be included in her practice of repetition, recovery, restoration — the view from the window is insignificant, she is indifferent, and discontented, for unhappily one cannot move and still have everything. When she is forced to leave a place, momentarily she mourns it, sees it as if for the first time, as lost. That is as close as she comes.

I remember walking down the road in Turkey, and being allowed to hold on to my mother's index finger. It was just right. We suited each other, briefly. The road was hot, dusty, sunny. I remember feeling fine, happy — alone with Mommy, on some small expedition. Endless.

Some of the time we were dressed like twins, although there were two and a half years between us. This made us both feel uncomfortable, nothing, neither dress could be called mine. It was worse for me, as I also got the identical hand-me-downs, growing. Nothing more dismal than growing out of a dress you never liked very much, only to grow into the same dress.

Doubling: we doubled up, uniform — the word was 'cute'. The eye was the mother's eye, the children without choice. My first fashion tragedy (so many yet to come) was when I grew too big for my party dress, and it was thrown away, no, more likely given away (even worse). It was white organza, with small flowers embroidered on it, full layered skirt (many petticoats), puffed sleeves, big sash. ('Come here, let me tie your sash.') It was a classic. I wore it when I was three. The tragedy was simply that although I knew I couldn't wear it any longer, I wanted to keep it.

There was a canary, when I asked what happened to it I was told Mommy had flushed it down the toilet. An image of desperate flapping, feathers and water, my mother's power, able to make the bird flush away. I never imagined it dead. (This story is not true.)

There was a dead turtle. It lay on its back, wet neck outstretched. The next day it was alive again. This was a miracle, but I suspected my mother had somehow in the night procured a new one.

There was a dead goldfish. I went to Woolworth's on Madison Avenue and bought a new one, exactly the same.

There was a puppy who was sick. They had it put down. This expression was new to me. It was my sister's dog, and they didn't tell her until she came home from school and said, where's Kelly?

Lost objects, parental position godly: she who gives and takes away. One Easter, when things were going badly, the parents close to separation, presents were produced for us kids. Guns, a superb gun, it was a small rifle, real metal (painted black) and wood, with a sound effect that was very realistic. BANG. Guns and bunnies.

In Turkey, in the winter, they went on huge sledding expeditions. It was unusual for so much snow to fall there. She remembered trying to walk through deep snow, putting my boots into holes made by my father, walking before me. Following in my father's footsteps. She could not make such steps. The snow almost came up to my waist.

Snow suits made a particular sound, a sort of swishing hiss, hissing swish, as your arms and legs slide against you, against each other. It is a specific soundscape, the snow on the ground muffles everything, changes the space, and then there is the crunch of boots in the snow, and the high distant cries of kids, and this delightful swish swish with each step. Her snow suit was red, she was very fond of it. Snow meant being bundled up to the point of impediment. It also allowed amazing speed — on my sled.

In Turkey, in the summer, there were massive expeditions: picnics. It was never hot, perhaps it was spring, all the kids had runny noses. We would drive, a small convoy, to a forest, a clearing. There were dead leaves making a spongy floor, large trees, muted sunshine through leaves, branches. There was a deep, wide ditch, with water black and murky in the bottom, green plants vivid around. Two waterbuffalo, big and black, stood in this ditch, or stream, like rhinoceri. Too big. Kids (small) were swung across the ditch, by fathers (large), to explore. The adults drank bloody marys, her father climbed a tree, went to sleep, and fell out. (This sequence reveals how young they were — thirty-two?) While the mother wiped our noses, fed us sandwiches, and us kids made adventures. Three year old, staring, transfixed by — a waterbuffalo.

I have, I found, I excavated a memory of being lost, in Turkey — that I think is a fantasy. I was frightened, as a small child, by the old Turkish · peasant women; they would exchange pleasantries with my mother, gesticulating, admiring, commenting on these cute little girls, and I would gaze wide eyed, until the gesture was made. She, dry wrinkles, hunched, too classically witchy for my comfort, would pinch my cheek, hard, shake my face, smiling. Such a gesture, it hurt, and yet it was affectionate, and teasing. Now I see a similarity to pinching good cloth, or slapping the hide of a healthy animal, appreciative, grasping health, wealth. You can't pinch the fleshy cheek of the undernourished Turkish kids. The gesture frightened me, it hurt, I knew it was meant to be nice, I was supposed to smile. It was like being teased.

I dreamed, I feared, I remember being lost — somehow. Wandering among muddy clods of earth, grass, no paved road, tracks, and the sod houses, like bricks, long, low, brown mud, with small windows, a fascinating poverty, frightening. These Turks were like gypsies, wild, colourful clothes, incomprehensible. I remember they made me come in to their house, and they found my father, and I was returned to my home. My parents came in a car, and took me home. I didn't cry, I was past that point, out further, simply completely lost. These strangers, I don't know how we spoke, but they stopped me, they kept me there, until the car came, rescue.

I was an absent, day-dreamy child, and I tended to wander off. I was lost in a department store. Later I was lost in the church, lost in the bowels of the church in New York, behind the scenes, I'd lost my Sunday School class, and the church itself, and I cried. A woman tried to help me. People got angry.

What it must have been like.

There is no clarity, no clear vision. Nightmares, fears, memories mix with what one has been told, retrospective pictures of what it must have been like. Obscured. I killed my sister, virtually, in a dream. My baby brother came home from the hospital, wrapped in a blue blanket. There was an owl in the shed in the field at the top of the hill. I don't remember any distance, what you saw when you looked out of the window, or when you got to the top of the hill. Always a difficulty when parents, Daddy, or Mommy, would try to point things out to me, 'Look —', and sometimes I would just stare, unseeing, and sometimes to please them, to soften their frustration, I would pretend to see whatever it was, a ship, a sight. I wasn't able to distinguish things, one from another, to tell what was to be seen. Although my vision (technically) was always good. When I recall Turkey, this little world, short vision, of four years old, the edges of my world were indeterminate, but close by. I don't remember what you saw out of the windows of our flat. That may partly have been because it wasn't easy to recognise. It was an American style apartment building set down beside a muddy field, on what seemed a big hill, a large grassy space, we sledded on it in the snow, we rolled down it in the summer, and I remember toiling up it to find the bigger girls, who hung out at the top, near the scary shed. It's hard to say now whether the shed was supposed to be inhabited by a ghost who made owl-like whooing sounds, or whether it was supposed to be an owl. My mind constructs (out of nothing) this scene: the bigger girls torturing the little girl, one hiding making the terrifying sound, and my sister and her friends saying it's a ghost it's a ghost, and me saying no it's an owl, only an owl. Later a sequence where the owl was as scary, more scary than the ghost, unravelled itself, so that now I am distressed (thinking of it), frightened of owls, in dirty broken down sheds. Yet I think someone lived in this house, a witch, a gypsy, a Turkish peasant, elderly — we were all scared of him, her. Another scene: the old woman comes up the hill, up the scattered marks of a rarely used track along the side of the field, and all the little American girls squeal and disperse, running away.

ROMANCE

BERLIN PIECE

Walking into the crowded café bar of the Kunsthalle, busy with International Film Festival, shy and ugly, to meet Robert, who was not Robert at all, Tracy said, quite unthinking, 'I didn't know *you* were coming', and there was some embarrassment. Slowly she realised that this was, indeed, the expected Robert, not (as she mistakenly imagined) Richard, and her announcement of her own faux pas still wasn't quite enough to cover the embarrassment, and slow realisation unfolding: that this man was Robert — and therefore the man on the phone to Rose last week, shouting, was *also* the utterly charming and amusing visitor to London of a few months ago, the man in the grey suit, who came to their house bearing a bottle of whiskey, and stayed to tell stories about New York and make them laugh. Tracy had hated the man on the phone shouting at Rose, and so imagined that the visitor in the grey suit must be Richard, since the creature on the phone losing his temper was indubitably Robert. (They couldn't be the same person.) So when she expected to meet evil phone screamer Robert, and instead encountered the charming man she thought of as Richard, in his grey suit, Tracy didn't pause to question this, but plunged right in, 'I didn't know *you* were coming.' And since the fight had been about who was accompanying the film to Berlin, this remark could be, and was (at least by Fran) taken to be an immensely aggressive lie. Tracy found herself in a tizzy, trying to figure out who this fellow was (did Robert and Richard look alike?), slowly like a machine that's got muddled, all the cards reshuffled, and dropped into place. She realised she'd never met Richard. Robert politely said they were mistaken for each other all the time. Tracy tried to make up for her gaffe by laughing at his jokes; it seemed to work. But she felt shy or nervous towards him.

Looking back, she thought she could remember finding him attractive, although she did not actually think that thought: her usual taboo. She remembered only her embarrassment and a concomitant desire to please. She remembered Klaus, the German film maker, claiming he knew her, some years back, when she was fatter. It was uncomfortable to be remembered, fatter, and not to remember. She remembered Fran sitting quietly, self contained, and Rose's slightly manic conversation, and herself feeling out of place, and very very tired. And then, finally, they went to eat: the three women, somehow, extricated themselves from these men, whoever they were, and found the Paris Bar, and ate, and became interested in what was happening there. And forgot Robert.

He was staying at a very expensive hotel, which Rose said Godard was always put in, and always pissed on the carpet (on principle). This Tracy found hard to believe. Kurt said, à propos Robert, 'How can I like someone who wants to stay at the Kempinski?' Fran later teased Robert quite aggressively: 'You're ruining my reputation as a radical film maker.' He was not in contact with them; this was double-edged: Tracy felt they'd been something of a gang of women (the three of them shared a cheap hotel room), necessarily excluding him, and at the same time she realised he'd been hanging out, and going to parties, and not inviting them — i.e. not wanting to cart around this caravan of three difficult women, who couldn't really even be counted on to be socially gracious. She got the picture: he was a snob, he knew how to have a good time, he was 'bright' and 'amusing', he was staying with his fiancée, rich New York career woman, at the most expensive hotel in Berlin: an attempted man of the world. At the same time he seemed — nervous, shy, never allowing silence, a divided social persona, impossible to fathom.

But this was fantasy, retroactive from the secret bedchamber self — if she'd never touched that, Tracy would not have found herself musing over his mysterious deep inner life that seemed to be contradicted, repressed even, by his passionately social exterior. She would simply have laughed at his jokes when he was around, and not thought much about this somewhat peripheral figure when he wasn't. Remembering, she was forced to admit she was fascinated by the Kempinski because she'd spent a night there; she envied his party-going in ways she did not while actually in Berlin, because she'd finally gone to a club with him and liked it. Memory shaped, and memory was shaped by the closure, the end of the story, as she reshuffled the elements of the beginning, into some kind of order.

Staring out the window in London, recollection in tranquillity, Tracy tried to make sense of this meeting, as snow gently fell out of a white sky, repeating the snows of Berlin, remembering. Everything conspired against analysis: it was a romance, even on the (real) level of weather. Pulling the pieces together, she performed an autopsy on this classic one-night-stand, a brave attempt to close the gate long after the horse had bolted.

They'd met the first night she arrived, and then Tracy didn't see him again until Monday, over a week later, at the screening of the film. There he indeed seemed excluded, sitting at a long table of ten women, talking, Kurt and Robert tucked onto a corner. He sat between Kurt and Laura, joking about England, nervous, not as nervous as Kurt, who was shaking — surrounded by Argentinian psychoanalytic feminists passionately discussing the film. Tracy listened, got roaring drunk, and eventually happily agreed to Fran's arrangement of her farewell dinner, this her last night in

Berlin. Feeling worser and worser, as Fran occupied their hotel room to write her last two paragraphs, deadlining, and Rose and Tracy sat, again, repetition, in the café bar of the Kunsthalle, drinking hard, and talking, talking with Kurt, Sam, Bill. She'd imagined Berlin would be like this, sitting in bars talking to men she didn't know, it suited her fine. Robert joined them, finally; he sat down next to her. And eventually they left this scene, they went to go out to dinner, walking in the night snow, to meet Fran — Tracy enthusing about childhood in New York, really happy, but feeling sick — wanting to drink more, to let go, but frightened by what amounted to a near faint in the Kunsthalle. Tracy felt that she was working her way up to some drastic feat of vulnerability, some act of self exposure. She felt it, and knew it, and wanted it — to do something, and yet she didn't see it coming, and she couldn't have allowed herself to think it, no, it was definitely out of the question. So it happened — passively, with Tracy surprised, and disbelieving, although it was what she wanted, and what she had, in some way, made.

CUMULATIVE EFFECTS

What happened was simply the rapid reshuffle of suspecting herself desired. The pleasure, further, of ignoring that secret, playing at not knowing, or if knowing, or, of course, only suspecting, acting as usual. The reply spoken aloud to the half whispered invitation, both obliterating the implications of the whisper, and, in some way, acknowledging them, water off a duck's back. Hiding her pleasure and her dismay, in the English fashion.

Critical, Tracy was amazed at her impression of this man: charming, amusing, intelligent — ghastly generalities, was that all she could come up with? From her table by the window in London, she realised she didn't want to know. To generalise his attractiveness, to locate his significance in things not peculiar to himself, was to counter the suspicion that her reaction had anything whatever to do with him.

The half whispered invitation, the reply spoken aloud — the implication that this man wanted to be alone with her ignored, quashed, acknowledged — all this came afterwards, in the late night snowy street, after the meal.

In the restaurant, she'd been feeling quite unwell, tired and queasy, and eventually mentioned a headache; whereupon he leaped up and swiftly reappeared with two aspirin, wrested from the world, for her. Tracy was flattered, mystified by such a gesture, and at the same time aware of the numerous Disprin in her bag. They ate, and talked, she found herself unfunny, and told her perfunctory anecdote about boat-naming in Hamburg with difficulty. These tales seemed so much more extreme, even violent, mad, when recounted to people she didn't know; the level of exaggeration, of excess is impossible to measure, there being no exterior norm, no disbelief or dismissal. And these stories weren't really about her at all, but about her family, a history of her positioning within the family, powerless. So she told about the champagne bottle that didn't break, and her jaws aching with smiling, and the Russian vodka — which was the original association — and it all seemed quite mad, especially the sex show. Her stories tended to be told telegraphically, for fear of boring with this socially graceless mode of anecdote swopping, and perhaps it was their minimalism, the exclusion of telling detail, that gave them their brutal quality. In any case, these family anecdotes upset her, she didn't feel on top of them, and they seemed unamusing, although possibly intriguing, if you have a penchant for raving neurotics.

Fran and Rose and Robert and Tracy — eating, talking, bitching at each other, laughing. Robert recognised a Dutch minimalist sculptor, whose catalogue, for a show in Flagstaff, he had just designed. He went to say hello to him. Tracy was interested in checking out the decor, the woman who ran the restaurant, and all the very fashionable people. Godard left;

Tracy didn't see him, Robert did. She ate fish with difficulty. There was some confusion when the rather large bill arrived. They had discussed how good looking the waiters were, Tracy liked the man behind the bar better than their waiter, who had thick straight clean black hair and a boyish face. Robert said he liked this one best, that he liked young boys. Then he said David Bowie would be the only man he would really like to go to bed with. (Did this win her heart?)

Their waiter was standing next to Robert, his back to him; they wanted the bill. Robert gently put his hand, flat, on the young man's bottom, right buttock, as one would gently touch a shoulder blade. The man turned, hands in air, camp but angry — 'all these hands!' The three women pounced, Fran saying Robert would have got a kick in the balls if *she'd* been the waiter, Tracy about to say the same thing, but inexplicably silenced, impressed, Rose initially condemning, quickly celebrating — and Robert protesting that he would not have done it if it had been a waitress, Robert claiming it was a 'non-sexual' gesture. The gesture was momentary, the memory of it almost slow-motion clarity: the coincidence of a transient, unconscious gesture and the chance looks of three women. They all saw it.

Again the sexual fascination was retrospective. Tracy remembered only *not* saying 'kick in the balls', and surprising herself — later she would attribute her silence with meaning, with parts of meanings. As Rose said the next day, the hand on the waiter's bottom was displaced eroticism on display, seen.

It was indicative of the slightly strained relations between them that Rose should have decided to walk home alone in the snow, rather than take a taxi with Tracy and Fran. She vanished. Then Robert muttered his invitation, and Tracy replied aloud: 'No, I think it seems a bit late, I'm awfully tired . . .' Then he mentioned the Dschungel, and she started to rope Fran in, 'What do you think?' Somehow it was out of the question to stagger off into the night with Robert without even putting it to Fran as well — Fran who still had work to do, who wanted an excuse not to go back, who would play gooseberry in this private drama of denial (denial that anything untoward, anything sexual might be going down). Tracy wanted to go, to the Dschungel, with Robert, and she wanted to deny the unusual aspect of the whole exercise, to displace the eroticism once, or twice again, and so she roped Fran in. It would have been embarrassing not to reply aloud: as if making the assignation for sex at the beginning of the evening rather than the end.

MODERN CONVENTIONS

The scene is set, the message shared: an initial incoherent statement, in the form of a muttered invitation, receives its ambiguous denial, by the inclusion of a third, as witness, chaperone, norm. Arranging her recollections, all of these gestures made by Robert were interpreted by Tracy in the retrospective context of a gestural progression, a systematic and somewhat clichéd pattern of seduction, that ends with the final gesture of orgasm. The isolated word, or look, or avoided glance, at the time, was fragmentary, out of context, ambiguous. But, this was the beginning, standing on a snowy, almost New York-ish street corner, about to hail a cab, and instead deciding to go to the Dschungel with Robert. Of course Robert said he was going whether they did or not; retrospectively the shift from 'Would you like to go somewhere for a drink?', to 'I'm going to the Dschungel', seemed part of the pattern of seduction. Did he remember that Tracy had said she really wanted to go there? Did he want her then, or only a woman to go out with, just not wanting to be alone? (The fiancée had gone back to New York.) Tracy remembered noting this shift, characterised by the spoken aloud, almost announcement intonation, as opposed to the tentative mutterings of moments before.

Obsessive, remembering, Tracy couldn't help but be aware

that most people, including this other, this Robert, prefer to forget these details, telling, speaking details. The modern convention of the one-night-stand is blurred, generalised: yes, it was fun, or O.K., or great. Who wants to follow the stage by stage, moment by moment enactment of a seduction? Who is it for? Certainly not Robert, although at the same time the thought, the question of what he would make of all this kept coming to mind. She suspected he would think she was in love with him.

The club was a venetian blinded glass shopfront, with central, inset door; there was no sign. The man checking coats wore a suit, circa Bowie 1973, thin leather gloves, and make up. Tracy sighed with relief, aware that she could rely on her dress. (Some concern, however, about greyish old brastrap showing — a gesture developed, gently pulling the sliding neckline back up her shoulder.) There was a gallery, with hi-tech stairs up to it, tables, a large bar downstairs, and at the back, an area of dancing, darker, and noisy with beautiful modern music she did not know. They took a table on the gallery, looking down onto the people; bright, though not unflattering light, the spaciousness, the carefully positioned mirrors, all emphasised visibility as the quality special to this place. Pleasure in looking somehow balanced out the usual (English cool) anxiety in being seen, both activities became pleasure.

Tracy woke up: an old feeling, an unfamiliar feeling — showing off. Display, the dress, the body — she was pleased even by the differences that set her apart from the extremely groovy Berlin scene. She felt older, detached, less insecure — without that edge of desperation, the need to be in with the in crowd. Her dress was an unusual shape, oddly sexy. She wore short suede boots, black stockings. She felt womanly, and young; desirable, and nervous; and as always, deep down, just funny-looking, aware of the necessity to exploit that, make it part of the display. Excitement started to generate out of conflict: desired but forbidden, nervous and knowing simultaneously.

Fran's presence was instrumental; she knew Robert well, having worked with him in New York, and clearly she was not at all susceptible to his charms. Thus she got Tracy into the place — and then went, leaving her happily stranded there, alone with Robert. This was very useful. It cannot be emphasised too often that Tracy felt like a housewife out on a jaunt, that had suddenly and most unexpectedly turned into some kind of seduction. Her feelings were a combination of surprise, pleasure, disbelief, and inadequacy. Hiding this successfully was impossible, obviously, so she didn't try, holding on to the old idea that the display of such incoherence (her bun, for example) would add to her attractiveness. It was the ancient tactic: confuse the enemy.

After a short time, Fran left; Tracy descended with her to go to the loo. Fran openly acknowledged that Robert was 'making a pass'; Tracy reluctantly, ironically admitted that this indeed seemed to be the case. They laughed about whether or not they would meet later, at the hotel — Tracy insisted that unless her whole scheme of things changed completely within the next ten minutes, she would definitely be coming back: sex was out of the question.

In the toilet Tracy saw the back of her head in a large wall mirror opposite, as she put on lipstick. She had not seen the back of herself in years. The bun looked enormous, very feminine, womanly even. It seemed a cruel contradiction of her self image, imagining she looked better, cool 'n' groovy, with her hair up, clean lines and that. Her long hair seemed domestic, depressed; putting it up, like putting on lipstick, was a sign of going out. Now her bun seemed grandmotherly. This was something of a shock: she fled, swiftly returning to Robert, more drinks, dancing, talking.

Watching: sometimes with one hand, he tapped the flat back of the other, lying flat gently on the table — a gesture of her father's, connoting boredom, irritation, nervousness. It made Robert seem manly. Inevitably Tracy was ambivalent towards the 'manly': it was fundamentally suspect. Its attraction was dangerous. But the pleasure of listening to someone who appeared to know what they want, know what they're talking about, know how to do: it was this myth of mastery that Robert represented for Tracy. His denial of doubt, assertion of simple self confidence, was interspersed with small references to tragedy (his own TB, a dying woman, a lost friend) — gestures to acknowledge a 'deeper meaning', which at the same time did not detract from his sheer determination to have a good time, now. It was an irresistible combination. Tracy, as usual, presented herself as the unvictimised victim, the chronic depressive flummoxed by living who is so dynamic not to say amusing in the telling that all that is thrown into question. She remembered talking about her family again. They had to almost shout.

She liked dancing; from the non-specific expression of (libidinal) energy to the specific gesture, towards one other, this slow movement from display to everyone and no one, to gesture for one other, and the lovely co-incidence of unconscious movement and display — only dancing does that. She kept catching people's eye — were they looking at her? She suspected everyone feels that, the fantasy of the dance floor. Eventually they were in each other's arms — very sexy. Even so, she held back, thinking of garden paths, and marriage.

Finally Tracy spoke, decisive:

'I really think I ought to be going I'm exhausted.'

'Would you be offended if I asked you to come and be exhausted with me?'

'No no not offended, actually I was going to say that if I — to suggest — I was going to say let's go back to your hotel room and fuck all night except that I am strictly monogamous, I have only slept with one other person in four years and I don't *do* this.'

'I understand yes of course.'

'So it's rather sad.'

'Yes.'

'Well at least the feeling's mutual,' she insisted, breezily.

'I didn't know you lived with someone in London,' he replied.

'I don't, I don't live with him but we're virtually married.'

'Yes I know what you mean, I know about that.'

They ordered their last drinks, (the waiter, bemused, brought a glass of milk instead of the bill, like in a movie, the last joke), and consumed them somewhat ironically, commiserating — this small misfortune, small obstacle to each other's pleasure, and their own. It was funny, charming, amusing, and deadly serious. This was her refusal.

In the taxi they kissed. Tracy said, 'Kissing in the back of the taxi?!' 'Yes,' he said. It seemed pleasantly unsophisticated. The taxi driver couldn't find her hotel. They continued kissing. She felt the world conspiring against her, or at least against her refusal. Dropped off on a far corner of Wittenbergplatz, out into the snow, she waved and realised within moments that she had no key. She had completely forgotten the key problem: the hotel was locked, in their new room, No. 42, there were only two keys, Rose had one, and Fran had one. Tracy had no key. She remembered when she should have remembered, viz. when Fran left the club. She felt caught out, exposed: it seemed funny. Robert had said, in the taxi, 'If you change your mind you know where I am.' She remembered this.

Tracy stood outside the pension and shouted. Cooee Fran Rose, she screeched, shouting out over and over. It was only 2 a.m., their room was at the front of the building, fourth floor, she couldn't believe they wouldn't hear her. The lights were out. She stood in the snow for a time, then, heart beating, giggling to herself at the 'inevitability' of it all, Tracy took a cab to the Kempinski.

In retrospect, it was agony. (It was agony to remember.) At the time it was seen to be unavoidable (she simply had nowhere to go), and exciting. They telephoned Robert's room from the reception desk; regarding her dubiously, they told her to go up. The hotel room was very expensive: muffled, with red roses, whiskey. He turned on the radio. (That one gesture encapsulated for her all the corny, agonizingly clichéd elements of this seduction.) She was shocked. Tracy sat on a straight chair, and attempted some kind of conversation for a few minutes. She commented on how neat his room was. She made a slip; suggesting that he too was monogamous, or at least not unattached, she elided the name Mary (his fiancée, whom she had never met) with the word married (quite easy to do). In effect, she accused him of being 'Mary-ed'. This was more aggressive than she had intended. Later she couldn't remember anything he said very clearly: something about not doing this very often. This was to reassure her. When she first arrived he said everything was up to her — he understood. Perplexing implication: that they could sleep together and not fuck? All that forgetting, those lost keys, would be for nothing? No — she wanted, (obviously), she must have wanted — a one-night-stand. With terrible irony, she plunged:

'So you want to do sex?'

'What, you mean like a line of coke?'

This repartee suggests a new verbalization for sex: to take sex, as people used to take drugs. Having sex is of course impossible, and fucking is exaggerated. Making love is specific to lovers. Making sex is O.K. but sounds like you are producing something. Doing sex sounds like doing a line of coke, so taking sex may be the one. It connotes taking a bath, a rest-cure, a holiday. It is good for you.

He said she was beautiful. She said let's go to bed and see what happens. She retired to the (marble) bathroom, washed her face, asked to borrow his toothbrush, he suggested she use his hairbrush, very polite. Her hair seemed quite naked undone. She got into bed while he was out of the room.

She could not believe he was not pretending. She told him later when they were making love, I cannot believe you fancy me. He told her he liked the way she talked. She could not believe this. She partly believed, she wanted to believe. At the same time, he showed signs of being surprised that she could so unselfconsciously demand statements, compliments, some kind of explanation for this amazing mutual attraction. She felt, in retrospect, that he'd felt compelled to come up with some adequate description of her attributes, of which disbelief at her disbelief was the easiest to simulate, and his subsequent attempt at a list ('I like your body, the way you talk') consisted more of mumbled et ceterae than clear statement. She didn't know who to believe: her own disbelief or his. She felt that her sexuality had been entirely consumed, swallowed up by her monogamy: this man's reaction was a shock of pleasure, a revelation.

They did sex for some time. Tracy couldn't come. It was clear to her that this was for emotional rather than physical reasons; she was shy. Fucking him was all about difference — he was not-Jim, more than he was Robert, or anything else. It was an adventure. Her orgasm, or lack of one, went unnoticed. His was noisy. He bruised her arm slightly, which she liked, a pattern of fingerprints found, later, sweet souvenir.

Afterwards she said, 'I feel like a little girl, can I have a drink of water?' Afterwards he slept and she came. Afterwards she could not sleep, hot stuffy heavy. She got up and had a crap. It was very dark in the room — she didn't like it. She waited for morning. She slept sometimes. She began to wonder what was going to happen. As the day approached Tracy thought, Tracy remembered that she would be seeing Jim at the end of this same day. She felt confused. She hated the hot dark stuffy room. She felt there was nothing she could do about it, she had no right to disturb Robert.

In the morning the telephone rang to wake him at 9.30. Tracy got up and took a bath. It was quick. She came back into the room wrapped in a white towel and sat on the edge of the bed where he was lying. He did not touch her. He did not move. She said, 'I expect I'd better be going.' He tacitly agreed. She got dressed and left, somewhat peeved not to have been offered coffee, a little shaken by his passivity. Was he frightened, shamefaced, regretful? Or just sleepy, insensitive.

In the elevator, she thought, why did he want to get rid of me, what did he not want me to see, what did he see in me? She'd said that she might see him at the screening later that day: she supposed it did sound as if she wanted to see him again. She imagined he was scared of that, didn't know how she might behave. What: throw her arms around his neck? Burst into tears? In any case this train of thought was not cheering.

Tracy felt absurdly conspicuous, standing in the elevator with all the respectable rich hotel guests, and swanning through the lobby in her scruffy old black coat. She was reminded of another hotel, years ago, another embarrassment. She was amused by her discomfort, in relation to Robert, and to herself. The snow was beginning to melt: she chose to walk home, taking short steps in her little ankle boots, conjuring up the fantasy of herself as Edwardian fallen woman, trudging home meditatively in the snow. She felt very young, very tired, delicate — and at the same time almost raucous, longing to get back to the girls and laugh, at her infidelity, her lack of coffee. At the hotel it almost became a theatrical display: Karyn sitting in the breakfast room with Rose and Fran, Klaus at another table, Tracy laughing, centre of attention, the naughty girl. She felt loved — someone said, this is only the beginning, and it gets better. She was amused, ironic, embarrassed, excited: showing off.

AFTERWARDS

That day, all day, Tracy's sense of excitement was acute and overwhelming. There was no place to put it, no name for it, no rationalisation. She couldn't stop thinking about it, talking about it, laughing. She wanted — to know what she was feeling. This definitely wasn't love: yet she really wanted to see him again — and didn't. He avoided her. (She avoided him.) Tracy didn't go to the screening of the films; he didn't come with Rose and Fran to meet her later. Tracy felt thwarted: so much wanting to see him vertical again, to modify, balance the bedfellow body sleepy thing — to see him as himself again, in that grey suit, laughing. But disappointment, and talk talk talk, Rose and Fran both very amused and sympathetic, not to say amazed. That evening early she got on a plane for London, alone, and arrived home to find Jim and Ella playing cards. By that time she was so tired the excitement had dissipated somewhat. Tracy told Jim almost immediately, unable to keep this sharp knife swallowed inside for a minute. Very hurt, that night he fucked her on the sitting room floor, anal, oral, reclaiming territory, punitive.

Soon Rose got back, and Tracy went on talking. Rose reminded her that Berlin was all about death, and ugliness. Tracy had seen herself on film the week before going, and had been horrified by her face, hair, gestures, teeth — wanting to protest: 'I thought I was much prettier than that!' She went to Berlin chastened, reminding herself that she wasn't very beautiful at all. That most other people were much prettier, and so on. Indeed she very nearly hadn't gone to Berlin: circumstances (primarily her analyst's absence) combined to make Tracy so despairing, suicidal even, the week before they were meant to go that she said she wouldn't, couldn't, that she was dying, she would fall under a car, she was incapable.

But later she felt better, and changed her mind, thinking she could always ditch her charter flight and spend a lot of money on a sudden plane, if things got rough. And on the plane to Berlin, at takeoff, she felt extreme fear, and slowly understood, in her panic, excitement and terror, that this was a time for all her death-wishing to come true — God would lean out of the sky and say: you want to die so much? O.K., you can die now.

While she was in Berlin Tracy told Fran about her acceptance of the inevitability of her own death: that every time she started to think of plans extending into the future, she would counter it with: — what's the point, you will be dead in six months, what's the point of even contemplating alternatives. It was a way of letting herself off the hook, very quiet, dull, everyday acceptance of the inevitability of suicide.

In London, feeling it out, she thought she understood; glancing out the window, she opened her notebook and began to write.

I want to record the peculiar quality of inevitability in this seduction, its blissful, infallible trajectory. The whole experience feels pre-determined, shaped by the one-way ritual of one-night-stands — and yet it was disrupted by a violent exhilaration that explodes the terms of that simple story. The disorderly excitement generated by such a predicament could be called love, but as I grow older, I am increasingly reluctant to write feelings off in the name of love — especially emotions that really bear little or no relation to the actual object, Robert, the arbitrary other. The excitement is like a little eruption, libidinal, an opening out of desire, without an object, only an aim. The object, this other person, is insignificant. The aim, blurred in the confusion, the surge of excitement, is narcissistic, repetitive, reductive — nothing to do with love.

The excitement that I felt the day after I slept with Robert was generated by the conflicts in my sense of myself as quiet, homely, chastened, and even duly dying — and my sense of myself as a live wire, mad, talking, flirting, sexy, surprised. It was a glimpse that change was possible, taking risks was possible — extremes, emotional extremes weren't necessarily those reached through despair. The laughter that comes out of me over and over again, is this the laughter of hysteria, a measure of my sense of spectatorship (watching me and R. doing this ritual dance, with variations), or of my pleasure? I suspect my feelings of pleasure are intimately bound up with feelings of watching and being watched. I had been seen — as very different to how I saw myself, and this active look had been enough to produce an alternative sense of myself, myself as I used to be — as someone who could, even should throw caution to the winds, and create myself anew (out of looks?) in some foreign city, like New York. I felt liberated, I felt indescribable: my usual vocabulary was inadequate to account for this state. And yet I dimly remembered it, from other times, places: the pleasure of illicit, risky, irresponsible sex — with someone you're never going to see again.

At the same time, I don't think the sex is terribly important, pleasurable though it may be. And Robert isn't important, except as a stranger and friend, a positioning rather than some personal definition. I can re-write that sentence: 'the pleasure of illicit, risky, irresponsible, sexy self-display *— with someone you're never going to see again.' Some contact, some exchange, but mostly merely the gift of myself, showing off.*

Of course I know taking off in aeroplanes is more like coming than dying.

The erotic excitement that rises to meet despair, at the thought of violent death, like the tears of self pity, is a kind of self-love, a kind of narcissism. Contemplating, fearing, expecting death are ways to explore self-love, to recite a litany of pain and loss that materialises the loved body. Fantasies of self-mutilation can become ways to think about the wholeness, discrete and complete, of the body, limbs, extremities: the perfection of fingers awaiting the cleaver, of white arms the razor, etc. Ways of looking at myself, from the outside, of appreciating myself negatively.

Passion trails thoughts of death, they go together.

My excitement was in passion exploding the poetics of despair, releasing images of action, freedom, power. For a day I was beside myself with excitement, before going home to my familiar, despair.

Perhaps the explosive contradiction was really between this complicated suffering, here, everyday, and the reductive, even murderous pleasures of Berlin. Narcissism, its positive and negative aspects. Wild analysis. Stop.

PINNING THE TAIL ON THE DONKEY

A year passed; Tracy re-read what she had written, critical, dubious, remembering.

The lady doth protest·too much — this writing seems an elaborate construction, defensive, to fend off the insinuation that she might be even nearly in love.

She asserts at the beginning that she is reluctant to write off her experience in the name of love. Perhaps she overdoes it: claiming this man was 'insignificant' (merely a memory of Daddy? — the tall man in the grey flannel suit), she denies him his reality, pretending it's nothing to do with him. This assertion is required by her project, which is the evasion of action: if he's real, she could see him again. She could pick up the phone. (I could?) She doesn't come clean: his 'effect' on her is understood solely in terms of the language of her symptoms, as an unlikely, disruptive intervention in the endless cycle of depression and anxiety. Yet denying this specific other his power to 'make her feel that way', to transform, is a precondition for this project, this refusal, this writing.

The writing attempts an analysis of conflict, whereas naming 'love' blurs contradiction, overwhelms analysis. Love silences, rushes in waves, sea over a rock; it erupts in giggles, sighs, tightening cunt, loosening bowels, the convulsive memory of the womb, the uncontrollable smile, rage. Love makes you shudder. She shudders. Denial makes you write — pages to explain away a shuddering.

The First Letter to New York

Dearest Fran —

All of my writing implements, varieties of paper, seem inappropriate — a terrible moment poised to speak, yet I must allow the erotics of writing, nothing gives me more pleasure except (sometimes) sex. A terrible frustration — I want to be speaking, not writing . . . can you gossip in a letter? (Traditionally that's what you're supposed to do.) Writing is such a trial, there is never enough space, or time — if I have any aesthetic at all it is going back over things, over and over, *variations*. And conversations spread and ripple, while writing creeps, a quick snake sneaking in scribbles.

I am in love.

This is wonderful to write. But there are better surprises, because it's partly (at least) a joke. A joke against myself.

First of all I am *not* rich and famous; stupid publishers haven't delivered; their 'invitation' (as I thought it) was merely a Disruption of the most distracting kind — and Waiting for Them to Reply was an activity that filled weeks if not months, until now when I am no longer waiting, but don't know whether to go ahead and attempt the project without them — or to go on with whatever it was I was doing when I was so *rudely* interrupted. Which was I can't remember I think at least thinking that my best energies should go into what I still can only call 'my own' work. The teaching continues, tediously, needless to say.

So my professional life is in tatters of confusion. I have a number of large projects that I never find enough time to start properly, begin — much less, complete. But this is (I suspect) a mark of wellbeing (altho' my friends especially Jim, are disturbed by me being what he calls *frantic* — does he mean manic or just busy?) — I tell myself it is better to have too much to do (as now) than nothing to do (see last 5 years), but I don't know what it means to be 'better'. I mean I'm still no closer to accomplishing anything, altho' I may be closer to desire.

Whom I am in love with is Robert who was in London a couple of weeks ago. I hope this makes you laugh. He and I had (did) another one-night-stand, the very last night he was in London, (you realise we hadn't seen each other since Berlin, over a year and a half) and the whole thing happened again, except this time round I didn't put it all down to some kind of arbitrary excitation — but decided it was him. *He* does this to me, this particular man (whom of course I have only spent time with in the most lively social situations, in which he shines, makes me laugh, gives me (everyone) a Good Time) — (so I have no idea what he'd be like in daily life) (so maybe it's fun dinner parties and going out dancing that I'm in love with, can't get enough of) — NO: this particular man I find devastatingly attractive.

This is because my (oh so sleepy) sexuality wakes up with a bang, because he's taller than me, and seems relatively rich, because he has a car and a job and lives in what you once described as the most beautiful loft in New York (is this true?), because he stays in a hotel when he comes to London, because he makes me feel utterly desirable and feminine and like I — what, I should marry him and have babies and live in New York and be glamorous and intelligent, and have a lot of *fun* in this short life —

Because he has 2 existential modes, vertical and horizontal (public/private, upright/in bed) and the conflict between them is endlessly frustrating, enraging, fascinating to me. He gets so close and then backs away so quickly, firmly. He seems (for me) the *classic* (frightened) male, all sensitivity and defense. He is 10 years older

than me. He is Daddy all over again — except a bit nicer
to me (though not that much). He evinces the fatal
passivity of the male, the kind that brings out the most
extreme violence/aggression/rage in me. Minutes later
he seems the only man who ever allowed me to be passive
(sexually), to sit there and lap up the attention he gives.

And the fantasy goes on —

All of this is Unreal — except that it's two weeks
(today) since he left, and my stomach still turns over with
desire when I think of him (although I don't think of him
all the time, as I did the first week). And it's so wonderful
to be alive with passion, so rare, I wonder if a) he doesn't
feel it; b) he does but much more often (i.e. it's not Me
that does it to him); c) there are Many women in his life
ETC. (Apparently he's bust up with the fiancée.)

What happened to *feminism*??

Even in thinking about him I come up with clichés —
'alive with passion', 'women in his life' — *what*? (You will
have noticed my list of his attributes describes the exact
opposite of Jim.) I'm incapable of measuring the extent to
which I invent this Other — or how much he overlaps
with my invention. But this time around, this run-in with
Robert, I am getting nearer to being able to recognize
that he is not a fictional character, a figment — he is a
real person, and if I want him I can go after him. (The
spectre of Action rears its terrifying aspect.)

And I am, of course, giving all this up. I think about it
when I'm alone, but gradually the well-springs of passion
are running thin, as I block them with the Realities of my
life, the impossibilities . . . and deny, and disavow, and
disallow, and deprive, and destroy my pleasure.

Needless to say, Jim doesn't like any of this. (But he
doesn't know the worst — the 'love' bit.) (The 'love' bit I
try very hard not to take seriously) . . . (I mean I'm sure I
could no more marry Robert than I could become a

doctor — or something — it's Another Life that I want, and it's infinitely retrograde because in too many ways it's Mommy and Daddy's life...) (What do I think — that he can wear the suit, and go to work, and I can be the woman. It's like playing house. It's positively primordial (Oedipal): I actually want to 'give' him babies!)

BASTA!

So I do laugh at all this.

Sometimes I think all this passion is just a ruse to distract me from work. Today I think, what work?

Write to me. I'll write again. I love you very much.

T.

The Second Letter to New York

Dear Robert,

This is for you.

This is what I wrote in a notebook, two weeks ago:

Dear Robert, Having found myself unable to get you out of my mind, I have made a concerted if intermittent effort to suppress my 'love' for you — as I attempted to analyse it away, last time.

Dear Robert, Having found myself unable to bear the loss of a desired object, finding each memory trace (trace?), finding each trace imbued with anguish (more, more, I want more), I have managed, this time round, to merely squash my attachment to you. It has been not unlike smothering a baby. My desire screams. I carry on a normal life, silent.

Dear Robert, Now that my desire for you has worn off a bit (time passes) I can talk about it a bit.
No I can't.

Dear Robert, At first, after we parted, when I thought of

you my body would shudder and clench. I was infuriated by my loss. Now, even, I get a pain behind my breastbone (when does one learn the word heartache?) when I think of all the things we didn't talk about. But it's too late for authentic emotion: as usual, the lost object is anonymous. Yet I do recognise *you* somewhere in the mish-mash. Last time I tried to say it was all my doing: 'you' reduced to a catalyst in my symptomatic structure (my structure of symptoms) allowing (rather than causing) a slight shift, quickly returned, nullified. This time I was forced to acknowledge (is this a measure of the success of my analysis?) that you are a real other, and I want *you* (not some figment of my history or my imagination). But I quickly nullified this also: by leaving our meeting to the last minute (the last night), making no time for the dangerous pleasure of finding out who you might (really) be.

Dear Robert, You gave me a gift (twice) of myself as I would like to be — doubtless a narcissistic thrill. What do I give you? (can) (did)

Dear Robert, I would like to give you this writing about you, though really it's about me, and you're too far away, now. I also want to maintain the cool façade you specialize in —

So there you are.
I didn't realise you lived in that street — I spent Christmas 75 there with Michael and have extremely vivid pictures (and I think, somewhere, actual photographs) of the green fire escapes in the narrow street opposite — with yellow sun — the view from that window. I think that was No.9.
This love letter is awfully solemn (and of course, sad, tentative, serious — like me). But I don't dare get

romantic — in case . . . I'd like to sit in a bar and get
drunk with you — and laugh and talk.

love, Tracy XX

On the phone

'I was fascinated by your letter.'

'Fascinated?'

'And embarrassed.'

'Oh well yes it is *very* embarrassing.'

'And then appalled — and then sort of — thrilled. And
somewhere between those four words is my — reaction.' He
laughed.

'Well I took it that embarrassed and appalled won out —
and I sympathized actually — although I sort of expected at
least a postcard or something, saying um I got your letter . . .
Perhaps I'll write you another one.'

'Yes that would be great, you can write to me, and I'll call
you up four months later.'

'Sounds like the perfect relationship.'

An Exercise in Reality Testing

When Tracy finally took action, and went to New York, in
pursuit of Robert, she fell in love with someone else the
minute she stepped off the plane. She found this new object at
a party, and (almost by accident) ended up going back to his
place, very tired, very late at night. Getting out of the taxi,
looking up, streetlight, she saw snow falling slowly out of the
black sky. Her fantasy so neatly displaced, it was easy to see
Robert as infinitely undesirable, a complete mistake. (Later
she would refer to him as a can-opener, an essential device to
extricate her from the relationship with Jim.) The new object

was: reluctant, brilliant, terrifying. Nevertheless she called Robert up; they had dinner.

Robert said: 'You think I'm a shit? I'm a shit, I don't mind.' (That was about business probably.) He told her feminism was 'irrelevant', it had been 'discredited', no less. She knew then that he wasn't trying to win her heart. He told her psychoanalysis was out of fashion; he made racist jokes, flaunting his success, his cynicism, superficiality. All surface, cold and smooth, she perched on his sofa, eating his perfect meal.

Tracy had arrived at his house upset, about Michael, their mutual friend, and junk — presenting him so to speak with an emotion — and he'd said: 'I don't know what you're so worried about, if Michael is going to kill himself, he's going to kill himself, there's nothing you can do about it.' She didn't say, that's precisely what's so distressing, but shut up, reprimanded.

They slept together, out of politeness. It wasn't pleasant. Cold as ice, no love, the glimpse of vulnerability, the wonderful contradiction (vertical/horizontal) was completely shut down. And Tracy was too cowardly (aware of how rude it would be, and of her responsibility for setting up this ghastly meeting — it was all her doing, it seemed) and, to an extent, nostalgic for her (distant) fantasies — her love for him — to be able to get up, and walk out. (And go see the other man, the one she really wanted to see.) So she stayed, out of etiquette (never again, never again) — and a sense of loss (the end of a story).

RELUCTANT

Gall and wormwood bitter in my mouth, I swallow the ashes of my will, I have made a burnt offering of my heart, and now I eat the ashes. White and dry, hot and dry, no liquid rush, no surge, I swallow hard, to stop it.

Artemisia was a queen, wife to Mausolus, satrap of Caria, in the fourth century B.C. When he died, she mixed his ashes in a drink and swallowed it, thereby making of her body a living, breathing tomb. This is probably untrue. She also built the Mausoleum at Halicarnassus, which was one of the seven wonders of the ancient world. If she ate her husband's ashes, who was buried in the Mausoleum? She was, I guess.

My heart is red and wet, it surges and pumps, it is like my vagina or my emotion. It weeps, menstruates, sweats, licks its lips, makes sex, or love. It is my strongest muscle, moving all the time, making time. My heart wanders, hysterical, it flies up to my throat, slips sideways, grumbles wetly in my bowels, and rushes with pleasure in my womb. It sinks to my heels, making my steps heavy, like lead in my shoes. It throbs, slow and deep, and then beats hard, quick and nervous, it makes me catch my breath. My heart sits like a throne in my chest, solid and wet, present and slippery, it's mine.

I gave you my heart, you didn't want it. It was too red and

*A genus of plants distinguished by a peculiarly bitter or aromatic taste.

101

wet. Back it came, weeping like a rock, exuding misery in dark drops. I pinned it to my sleeve, bravely, but it quickly lost colour, and began to decay. Like Isabella, I wanted to keep this pain near me, wet in black earth, I wanted to grow it, weeping. I was in danger of drowning.

Hot and dry, gall and wormwood, I burned my heart to ashes, and drank it down. I froze the liquid rush of love, stopped it, and obliterated my tears, signs of life, in fire. I stopped it, and then I destroyed it, and then I swallowed the ashes of my love.

It no longer appeared. You were relieved. You knew none of this had anything to do with you, you knew it was a matter between me and my heart. You hadn't killed it, I had. Hot and dry, burnt out, that wet pumping rush was gone, at last.

But what you don't know, is my body became a living, breathing tomb to my love. The ashes remained, bitter tasting in my throat, while fire curled through my nerves, my limbs — and I lived a mourning, the whole of me a mausoleum, containing the ashes of my heart.

His lip was crooked, a slight twist, trace of the split mouth, cleft, a tiny scar. His eyes, grey, were slightly too close together, hidden behind glasses and forward falling hair. His face was conventionally good looking, the eyes and mouth made it beautiful — flawed. His voice was low, he sat hunched, gesticulating, a smile hovering, rippling across his sentences like the momentary physical inscription of pleasure; his words were charged, excited. He delighted in a scenario of intellectual pursuit and seduction, a passionate flirtation played out in conversation only. His arrogance was without measure, his narcissism beyond remedy. His slouching stance belied a strong body, occasionally it struck, a young man, perfect. He was rich, he was very clever, and without doubt.

His passivity (sexual) was the obscure counter to his feverish activity (intellectual), endlessly generating words, ideas, play. When he stopped, it was to revert to the passivity of the infant, who takes and takes with the intensity of a profound reluctance, who submits to pleasure with difficulty, his gestures tracing ambivalence, conflict, withholding, whose orgasm is made out of rage and refusal relinquished, passionately. His pleasure is taken. There is no gift.

I present myself to you in all my vulnerability. This is deeply threatening. It's a battle to the death, your control against my passion, your cruelty meeting my will to suffer. It is maternal, my position, it is powerful. I have this thing to give you, this love, this understanding. I want to lie down like a pancake, flat and soft, and say, walk all over me. (But then possibly I am most powerful, most myself, in this position.) Calling it 'giving' is mistaken. But it's not 'taking': that would threaten *me*.

When I really get confused is when I ask myself, what do I want? The cozy thing about rejection is that it never raises that issue: in love, I simply *want*. You don't want. That's what makes it simple: I want you to want me. I imagine that I would stay with you forever, that I would always want you. It is more straightforward when you are absent. Your presence presents difficulties, complicates: I no longer want you, I want sex with you, you (amazingly) seem to want something with me, but it's not sex. We tend to have an unpleasant time. That night on the telephone when I was drunk enough to fight with you, you said you enjoyed my company, and I said Ha! really, really, do you? I don't enjoy seeing *you*. Giving myself away, risking all, (this strange friendship) for the chance of some kind of resolution. It resolved nothing. Here I sit, at my desk, going over and over the same ground.

Walking home, keeping tears under, an internal interrogation going on, an attempt to account for this devastation. Sitting down alone in my white room, doctor and patient, I question myself, testing the damage, gingerly. How are we going to describe this one?

Can we be bitter? Can we formulate a biting, sour tone — allow irony? How serious is this? Can we kid me out of it? Twist the tension tighter 'til it breaks, a burst, a bark of laughter. But it isn't funny, not when suicide seems sane. Short and bitter.

She is not sad. She is past being hurt. She is destroyed. There are no tears. There is no place for mourning, melancholia. There is stark, brute death: her face flattened by a brick, she cannot think. Blank, staring, dazed she is forced to admit this can't be a good thing. Trying to revive, internally she solicits tears, no response. Turning from tearfulness to irony, she tries to resuscitate her sense of self — to focus, a little clarity. Distance. Brutalized, she revives, if she can't feel sad, at least see the joke.

Mustering her defenses, she brings the machinery of analysis and understanding into play. A substitute for anger, she remorselessly turns it on her enemy, her friend.

This is the ritual, a ritual with slight variations:

Version 1:
We arrange to meet, and it turns out he has something to do
— some kind of work, with others, that would allow an
observer. I decline. We do not meet.

Version 2:
We arrange to meet; we meet and he announces his friend will
arrive because there is some kind of work they have to do
together, work that will allow an observer. I watch.

Subsidiary elements:

a hierarchy of exclusions:
    a. talking of books one has not read, or cannot read,
    because 'untranslatable'.
    b. talking of social occasions where one was not present.
    c. talking of future social occasions to which one is not
    invited.
    d. naming various other women, some known, some
    unknown.
    e. speaking on the telephone at length to un-named
    others.

sexual aggression:
    a. the jocular, biting reference to other men with whom
    one has any connection, as if to mention them is to make
    a joke.
    b. 'that was a light embrace' — aggressive passivity.
    c. 'come and see me *any* time, some afternoon, after
    midnight' — false flirtation.

intellectual aggression:
    a. conversation made up of contradictions (in the
    colloquial sense), making an argument, in which one is
    forced to defend a position — and fails. Instead of

exchange, there is only competition, or theft.

b. 'you *can't* like' — whatever it is one has expressed enthusiasm for.

c. 'you *must* know' — whatever it is one admits ignorance of.

d. your work falls into the category of what 'you *can't* do'.

Unrequited love: a protection from relation, sex, touch. 'It is very very dangerous to so touch another.' Therefore, a pursuit of rejection. A fascination with the resistance of the other: wanting someone so much, a wish to become the other, to incorporate him. Penis envy, and sexual obsession. Finally an inability to give up the wish, even when an actual relation transpires, where he can be recognised, critically, where the desired object is proved to exist in fantasy only. Hanging on to the wish like grim death, she resists giving up this possession, a possession not of the other, but her possession — her passion. A refusal to let feelings move — she wants to hold this wish still in her hand, like a weapon, powerful. It is the state of being in love she insists on sustaining — want, anguish — it is not relation she desires.

'What', asks Freud, 'does the woman [the little girl] want?' All the answers to the question, including 'the mother' are false: she simply *wants*. The phallus — with its status as potentially absent — comes to stand in for the necessarily *missing* object of desire at the level of sexual division.

> Juliet Mitchell: *Feminine Sexuality* (1982), p.24.

The term 'Penisneid' crystallises an ambiguity which may be a fruitful one, and which cannot be disposed of by making a schematic distinction between, say, the wish to derive pleasure from the real man's penis in coitus and the desire to possess the phallus . . . Freud also points out how the woman progresses from a wish for the penis to a wish for the man, leaving open the possibility of a 'temporary regression from man to penis as the object of her wish'.

> Laplanche and Pontalis: *The Language of Psychoanalysis* (1973), pp.314, 301.

At no other point in one's analytic work does one suffer more from an oppressive feeling that all one's repeated efforts have been in vain, and from a suspicion that one has been 'preaching to the winds', than when one is trying to persuade a woman to abandon her wish for a penis on the ground of its being unrealizable. . .

> Freud: *Analysis Terminable and Interminable* *S. E. XXIII*, 1937, p.252.

(You have red welts on your neck and arms. You have a delicate rash on your stomach, inside arms, behind the knees: as you say, the spongy bits. You have a receding hairline to the point of premature baldness. You have acne marks on your face. You have suicide scars on your wrists and inner arms. You have lines around your eyes — ravaged, not haggard. He has none of these.)

I present myself to you in all my vulnerability. This is deeply threatening. It's a battle to the death, your control against my passions, your cruelty meeting my will to suffer.

My flaws are interior. Your body too perfect, flaws manifest in language, gesture, your blurted cruelties, your silences.

The flawed body: forgiven. Sex as the forgiveness of the flawed body — each body so different, flawed in its own inimitable way — precise, perfect. My flaws are interior — physical, or psychic. The red wet inside going wrong.

To kiss his red welts, her scars, to love a flawed body, forgive. Sex infuses my body, transforms it. It's like a fire; it takes these weaknesses and makes them strengths. Suffused, a flickering light, lambent. My needs become beautiful, for the time being. My pleasure beyond revulsion, anonymous, greedy. Not very polite, but deeply friendly, generous.

Your refusal of sex makes my demand obscene. In the morning you told me I looked haggard. Ravaged, I said — ravaged, not haggard, dear.

When I threw my shoes at your head, I threw black high heels with all my strength across your big room, you ducked, laughing. Was that a play fight? I never fight lightly. My appalling bruises would seem to imply a seriousness on your part. But later you called it a pillow fight. I choked out a laugh.

Sex is never casual for me. It is always serious, it makes meanings. The minimal meaning is this bodily love, that forgives. Sometimes that is enough.

I wanted to climb into your dark bed, make love, fight, forgive. Knowing this your reluctance whelmed — you will flirt endless, come after me when I withdraw my (passionate) attentions, you will show me off, and put me down, and never never will we do that again. Over, over turning.

Nothing so crude as blows were exchanged. You never hit me, I think. It was so late at night, your dark room, we screamed in low voices, arguing. You never made a fist, hit me. We made love.

Yet our meeting hurt, bruised. Your will to humiliate me met opposition: I fought back, almost sure of the dignity of desire, willed vulnerability. The next day, in the full-length mirror alone in Evie's apartment, I found a pattern of violence on my pale body, the shadow of your grip imbued my white flesh with colour, finger marks like ink stains on my arms, black yellow and green dappling my breasts, the triangular fragment of a black eye. I put some Erace on the eye, and decided to forget you, rigid with shock, my body like an empty house, exhausted. You tracked me down, at my mother's house — at my mother's house, where I couldn't undress, where I couldn't wash my hair in her sink, where I couldn't expose these arms so incessantly black and blue, love, you called me up, and won my heart. I fell, felt, something, else.

Nothing so crude as blows were exchanged. More like accusations. I remember your cris de coeur, accusations of imperfection, inability. You don't understand. All the women, mother sister lovers, who'd betrayed you, disappointed you, misinterpreted. I don't understand. I stood in, whipped girl, for them all. And claimed, of course, that I did.

I still don't know where those bruises came from. When we were fucking, you said, come come *come* — and I came, hard, with you. Your words met my body, collided with my desire, left marks.

Finding a metaphor, I come up with images of torture, interrogation, confession. It is as if somewhere I see you as my inquisitor, enjoying the questioning, twisting the tension tight. I am found out. The only thing I have to withhold from you is the knowledge of my pain. I imagine you truly sadistic, making connection with yourself via the pain of the other. I imagine you torturing me. And me wanting more, more. I am almost surprised, by the persistence of this metaphor. Almost.

There's a sort of blankness, a state of lack. It is as if one doesn't know what to stretch one's hands out for, they hang open by my sides. I double up with sudden pain, but the blank seeps through me again like a gas: death-in-life. It is silencing; I am powerless. Time passes in bits and pieces, no sense, no sensations. My desire has been erased: I am left with smudged blank paper, disappeared.

Into this state a possibility arises: to meet. Desire revives, pushes like a terrifying plant through the cloudy wastes, pressing, urgent. The front of my body, my face, shivers, twitchy. I wring my hands, paint my lips and eyes, trying not to smile.

Imagining your eyes on me, I shudder with pleasure.

Lying in this heat I dreamed we were fucking. I was on my front, somehow, I was standing in the kitchen, you were behind me, you were naked, and your body was smooth and golden. I was doing something, the dishes, or cutting something up, you touched me, skin to skin, your penis limp grew hard, quickly you slid into me from behind, laughing, easy — I wasn't comfortable, easy, lying on my face on the kitchen table. Very close to you, your breath on my neck, I was worried about contraceptives, but I didn't want to stop, knowing your reluctance, if we stopped, found a bedroom — you wouldn't want to go on. The kitchen door was open, other people could walk in. Very close to you, near, I wondered if this was the time to tell you, as you gently fucked me, that you needn't worry about catching a disease. I was scared you would stop (remembering) — I wanted you to stop (to put my diaphragm in, to climb into bed) — I wanted this to go on forever. We fell apart, separate, somehow, people came in, or our mutual ambivalence (your reluctance, my distraction, discontent) slowed us down. Not that I could move, anyway. You unintentional, casual, holding me passive anxious longing, wanting something else from you, but unable to say no, to refuse myself this approximation of pleasure. It's rare to come in dreams, like dying. We didn't.

There is an intersection — of feminine illness — that occurs where my body makes pleasure, makes sex, makes love. There is a crossing, a junction, a conjunction — where blood meets come meets discharge rank meets the discharge, the shudder of my coming. Where mutating cells border on cancer, shift, scar. Where opened womb bleeds at the wrong time, gentle protest. Where fungus proliferates, given half a chance, a little acid shift. There is an intersection — of feminine illness — that occurs where my body makes pleasure, makes sex, makes love.

It hurts. It hurts to remember the pain of the three IUDs — put in, taken out. It hurts to remember the ache of the abortions and the imaginary children I don't have. It hurts to remember the pain of the sex that represents this suffering — the sex that is about pain.

The times I have been open mouthed on the floor, rocked in spasm. This is called period pain. When I have taken strong painkillers, and told myself to wait, bear the pain for half an hour, fifteen minutes, while they take effect, unbearably. When I have descended on hands and knees, ass in the air — the 'washerwoman position' — to aid my retroverted uterus in its convulsions. When I have held a clot of blood like black jelly in my hand, sitting in the bath, moved by its size, a great gob, to sense my life, my death.

Diethylstilbestrol, when taken by a pregnant woman, makes babies with funny vaginas. The kind of cells that belong in the uterus, internal, form the skin that lines the vagina, confuse the cervix. As you get older, these cells change, slowly scarring, becoming more like membrane, less like a womb. I picture it as being slightly turned, turned slightly inside out. The cancer comes when the shift, the changes go wrong. Meanwhile the cervix is a funny shape — 'deformed' — and the psychic representation is confirmed: damaged. Feminine damaged.

The anaesthetist said to me: when you wake up it will feel as if you've been kicked in the stomach by a horse. I imagined a horse's hoof, shod, my stomach. When I woke up it felt like I'd been kicked in the stomach by a horse. Precisely. There was some satisfaction in a metaphor so accurate. Pleasure that words could mean, connect this soft flesh, and icy floating mind. I held on to this, curled in a loose ball, cradling my scraped womb.

Internal external: penetration. They take sharp metal, and venture into my remote recesses, and pry open my body, to scrape out, suck out a little sac of cells, tiny frog, wet, alive. They count the fragments to check they've got it all (or is that just propaganda?). Minute, complete, the foetus is torn to pieces, discarded. They save my life. They give it back to me. I don't want it.

The difficulty of naming, the contradictory discourses of the body, the manifestations, that do not always interconnect, that won't make sense. There are unconscious mental processes, dreamy, a visual language. There is warm body, full, a silent partner, a house, a fact, myself. And there are words. Their intersection (kicked in the stomach) makes sense, makes the world mean. Holding my stomach, holding on to myself, holding on to a phrase.

Wrestling. It's a struggle to the death — the death of desire. Now that I don't want you anymore it is like a fire has gone out. I look forward to years of barren desert. What was important (it seems) was to feel desire — that was what I didn't want to give up. I held on to my love for you like a dying man's last hope. Now that you are gone I feel nothing, I feel different.

Late night. Your voice sudden, like a blow. (Felled by a sudden blow.) I quail, flinch, (my reluctance slight, like a wound). My body anticipates pain, reflexive — I stiffen, flicker, attending. Your kind words a sweet cocoon, deceptive, razor blades inside. Your pleasure lies in hurting me, mine in suffering you. My voice qualmish, thin, as I try not to give in, as I hide my distress, cover. I pretend — perform — imagining that in this way I deny you satisfaction. Childish I have no other way to hurt you than to suffer and remain silent. That is my revenge. That you will never measure the depth of my longing, the success of your schemes, the wet wound you have made in my chest. I will not let you know.

Thus we circle each other, your sharp instruments increasingly refined, cutting deep, exact — my camouflage a passivity like bandages, (while somewhere I am feverishly working to stop the bleeding, sew the cut). As long as I hide from you, you will persist — pursuing that peculiar delight of judging your work, contemplating the effects. While I can half pretend that I am not hurt, that my wish is not deathly. This is not torture.

Once you told me, eyes glinting, that more than one of your ex-lovers have confessed (under duress, you said) to telephoning and hanging up as soon as you've said hello. You said, to see if I was home. I knew it was to hear your voice. Sudden.

When I sit solitary, so late at night, sitting at the kitchen table, glancing at the paper, my mind turning over the evening, what we said, the telephone rings, sharp — I pick it up (it is right there), knowing it's you, no one else rings me so late. Your voice meets my delight, my defenses rise, and later my bruises — I press them gently, to test the extent of the damage, no nothing broken, only bruised. Unhappily I am forced to refuse your invitation to dinner (prior engagements), I am keeping talking, like the victim of an interrogation, trying to avoid confessing, keeping talking, and at the same time treating myself for bruises and shock, under cover.

'Bye — and the silence leaves me stranded, flailing, I reach and turn. Drawing pictures, I forget. And sleep, at last, to dream, as it seems I tend to, of you.

The first few days here my wish was so intense that I — walked down these streets with you, and couldn't really understand why you weren't here with me — it didn't make sense. Accompanied by your ghost, I showed you where I live. Now you are much more insubstantial (glimpses, and touch, I recall), but the gap this writing represents (that I cannot turn and see your face) is still intolerable.

To write the shudder, the deep quiver of embarrassment — a physical sensation, bound up with sexual shuddering, a sense of nearly intolerable exposure.

Anguish, like being flayed, excoriated. A scraping.

Embarrassment like a sea anemone, fleshy, quivering, or quaking, deeper. Embarrassed to tears, when the body folds up with a jerk, the mouth tears open, a groan emits itself. Or the short, almost piping 'oh, oh' that accompanies the embarrassment that can barely be laughed off.

Is there a pleasure in embarrassment? Wriggling. It is childish, the wriggling giggle that saves the sensation from veering out into agony.

All of this is solitary: the dialogue, narcissistic, with oneself. Acutely self critical, depressive, while at the same time amused, interested: a narcissistic alienation. It is entirely different to be embarrassed in public. This usually occurs because one has made a mistake, revealed an ignorance, transgressed some expectation or other. Here the sensation is fugitive, one spontaneously wants to get away, disappear, flee the subject, the situation. Knowing that the best way to overcome embarrassment is to acknowledge it — quel faux pas! — can seem merely a further brutality to one's tortured sensibilities, for this generous gesture is too often beyond one's strength. Unable to absent oneself, fast talking provides a certain psychic camouflage, although this can merely extend one's sense of unwilling exposure, as the frantic flicker of the cover-up reveals the depths of one's discomfort.

My love for you embarrasses me.

When I think of meeting you, anxious anticipation, over-excited, I start to quake.

St Agatha wards off earthquakes, and other natural disasters. The veil of St Agatha holds back the lava pouring out of Etna, and preserves the city. When the earth starts to fissure and shake, one calls on St Agatha. Her name echoes in shrieks.

St Agatha was a noblewoman of Catania, who took a vow of chastity in the name of Christ. Subsequently, she was pursued by the local Roman governor, and when she refused him, she was thrown into a brothel — whether this was intended to humiliate or to corrupt is unclear. Her virtue remaining unscathed, St Agatha was subjected to various tortures, to encourage her to change her mind. Finally her breasts were cut off, and she died. Her death was accompanied by earthquakes.

In paintings, she fixes the viewer with a seductive gaze, gently pressing a light cloth to her chest, its edges slightly tinged with red. Her shoulders and neck are bare. These paintings are about that space between the neck and breasts, that area of carnal implication. In these images, she seems profoundly aware of her sexual power, she is shameless. It is as if her martyrdom were a displaced sexual violation: she is unchaste, and yet saintly. Wherein does her pleasure lie?

It is rare to see a depiction of the act of mutilation itself: she is shown after the fact, transformed. Her death is chosen. The cloth does not reveal her wounds: this violence is a memory, elicited by the traces of blood, an idea in the mind. Without the knowledge of this story, the paintings would seem irreligious, erotic, a half-dressed woman confronting the spectator with her sexuality. The earthquake is also invisible.

When I think of meeting you, anxious anticipation, over-excited, I quake — silently. We collide, polite enemies. Our partings are catastrophes, I am left howling, stunned. With you I sustain an elegant appearance, my lipstick immaculate, while my heart fails me. I am sure this image takes you in, though my

123

pale face flickers with shock, my eyes recoiling, heart broken. I am devastated.

It was a picture of St Agatha I sent you, on Valentine's Day, last year.

Every martyrdom is chosen, celebrating victimization. Counting my wounds, I take power, invisibly. This is the pleasure we seek.

THE OTHER WOMAN

THE ANALYST'S BABIES

When Tracy left analysis, after four years of analysis, day in, day out, when she finally left analysis, her analyst said, 'Think about contempt.' A parting, poisonous gift she couldn't use.

The analysis had been interrupted by the analyst having babies. It seemed humiliating, to find herself subject to such inappropriate fecundity. The analyst was too 'strict' to simply say — I'm pregnant, I'll be taking this much time off, what do you think. Instead, the analyst would get larger, apparently hoping Tracy would notice, which she did, eventually. The first time round, Tracy spoke of an image she had of the analyst wearing trousers, gardening, perhaps, with her father. (The analyst's home address was 'Garden Flat'; on one of the few occasions Tracy had telephoned there, a man had answered the phone; clearly she lived with her father.) The analyst spoke: 'Have you noticed that my clothes have changed lately?' The reply had to be yes. The analyst's clothes had shifted slightly, from shapeless dresses towards shapeless smocks. It was possible that she was merely putting on weight. (Needless to say, she never wore trousers.) A week passed (five sessions) before the analyst finally admitted that she was indeed pregnant; she kept saying how necessary and valuable it was to explore all the ideas engendered by this putative transformation. The suspense was terrible. Nearly two years later, the analyst again made an uncharacteristically forthright

intervention (her silence was usually unremitting); deliber-
ately, the analyst suggested that Tracy never looked at her
enough. She was quick on the uptake: 'The last time you
mentioned your appearance you were pregnant; are you
pregnant again?' Furious, and determined she would not once
again play out the absurd game of is she/isn't she (alternatively, does she/doesn't she), the next morning Tracy refrained
from lying on the couch, and looked hard at the other woman,
who cowered slightly in her usually safe, invisible seat. Tracy
was aware that *she* hadn't made the analyst pregnant, that
however significant the parallels — Tracy lacked a garden, a
father, a husband, a Laura Ashley smock dress, a career, and
as for babies, her line was — I'm never going to have kids,
probably, and mothers, she'd watched childish as her mother
swelled and produced, waxed and suddenly waned — all this
was deeply resonant, the analyst's plenitude measuring her
deficiency, recalling her infancy, and so on and so forth, but
she'd been through this movie *once* already en analyse, twice
seemed more than excessive.

Struggling over the terms of her analyst's maternity leave,
together they managed to produce an ending. She left
analysis, or 'anal' as all her friends called it. She preferred the
diminutive, 'shrinkage'. Think about contempt, her analyst
said, her parting gift.

Tracy was devoid of opinions on contempt. What she
thought about was fear: fear that the analyst's expansive body
would burst open, that she would go into premature labour,
that there would be a mess in her uncomfortably neat office.
The analyst appeared oblivious of this risk, as if unaware of
how messy labour could be. Deeper than these, and more
pressing, was the fear that Tracy would damage the baby. The
foetus would become monstrous, violent, teeth and claws, a
nightmare, as an effect of her words, the sound of her voice
travelling through the analyst's body, into her ears, sliding
along her nerves, to pass through the soft placenta and wreak
untold aggression. She felt it was necessary to protect the

analyst's baby from her nasty thoughts, not only relatively unconscious thoughts about the analyst's baby, but all her wanderings, her words could kill, deform, distort, if she went on speaking, if the analyst went on sitting there, saying nothing, taking it all in.

She'd been through all this with the first analytic baby, anticipating its death, she looked to see if the baby seat was in its place in the back of the analyst's car, as she left after every session. She knew they would take the baby seat out, when the baby died. Occasionally doubtful, Tracy would remind herself of the people she knew whose babies had died, and once again validate this test of her anxiety: not dead yet. The (first) baby was still connected with the garden and the analyst's imaginary father — but when the analyst fell pregnant again, she moved house, and that image receded, it was not replaced. Tracy was never told the analyst's new home address; she imagined this was to ensure that she did not commit acts of terrorism, throw bombs through the nursery windows, or just moon about outside.

Tracy thought she would go to New York, in pursuit of love, and work, while her analyst took time off to have her second analytic baby; she figured they could both use a break. But they wrangled over dates, and money, and in the end she left.

Not long after she arrived in New York, a giant panda gave birth on TV. She seemed to be in a concrete cell, with no straw, or other warmth or padding visible; it appeared to be a concrete box containing only a giant panda invisibly in labour, and a video monitor. The minute infant, very foetal, was expelled from the mother, standing impassive on all fours, and immediately dropped three or four feet onto concrete. The scene was shown repeatedly on the news. The infant died a few days later.

In New York, Tracy got in touch with a woman that she'd been friends with in school when they were eight or nine years old. Her school friend turned out to be a pregnant psychoanalyst. She was married to a man who made advertisements for liberal politicians. They were rich and happy. They went jogging in the park every morning. Tracy was living downtown in a sublet above a greasy spoon with no natural light whatever. The loft was cluttered with very large sculptures of indeterminate animals doing sex. They didn't see each other very often, but when the baby was nearly ready to be born, Tracy was extremely fearful that something would go wrong. She was very relieved to hear that the little girl was perfect. In a department store, she looked for a gift to take to the baby: a small, stuffed animal. She found one that seemed infinitely superior to all the rest, that seemed infinitely desirable, that *she* wanted. Giving it to her friend, in their perfectly over decorated upper west side apartment, surrounded by her successful friends (including at least one other pregnant analyst), Tracy said, 'Isn't it sweet? You see, it's a baby giant panda.' As the words came out of her mouth, she heard what she had done, and began to cough, laughing.

The pregnant psychoanalyst survives intact, producing the good baby, no damage, no death. By taking herself far away, Tracy was sure she'd done the best thing, protecting the analyst's baby from her wishing, protecting herself from terror. She left with suitcases heavy with nastiness, all the stuff she had to keep from this fecund gardening married analyst, this good mother. It was unfinished business, but it seemed impossible to take care of, to work through. She was left with contempt to maintain the line she had drawn, the line between Tracy and these other women. She placed herself on one side — on the side of illness, abortion, the side of the deadly deformities, gynaecological horror stories, despair — in order to keep *them* over there — women with husbands or fathers or babies — to sustain the fiction of a healthy, happy femininity, a feminine body undamaged.

FAMILY ANECDOTES

For Christmas, my father gave me a set of four knives. Carbon steel, they were heavy, greasy, and wrapped, for safety, in newspaper. The largest was like a short sword: the blade was 12 inches long, and very broad. There was an eight inch one, and a boning knife, stronger, with a curve. Finally a little knife, paring. They were all very sharp indeed. I had asked for a knife to chop parsley.

That same Christmas my step-mother gave me a reticule: a disco bag. It was dark red leather, soft, woven, on a long string, to hang, symbolic pocket. I exclaimed: oh a vagina just what I've always wanted.

I was stunned by my father's overkill, and carefully took the largest knife, and the boning knife, back to the shop. When I told him this, laughing I told him I was too frightened by these knives to use them, and besides I wasn't that serious a cook, he said, angrily, but that's what you wanted, you asked for a vegetable knife. Instead I got — an enamel colander, a jug, a cake tester. Harmless.

But when I thought of coming to New York for a few months, I — I would invariably think, I must take my knife. I restrained myself.

But when I got here, I looked at knives, to buy. I didn't buy any: none were quite right. It seemed a bit excessive. My wish embarrassed me.

Then I dreamed — that I was still wanting, to buy a sharp knife, one really sharp knife. In the dream I opened a drawer and there they were, surprised, a set of knives.

I found the pearls in my mother's bedroom, we were playing out a scene of girlish intimacy, something that had been impossible when I was a teenager; nearly thirty now, we could talk about leg waxing at last. I sat in her room, as she did her face, my attention wandering, finding her jewel box lying open, pearls. I have never been drawn to real jewels before, the category is closed to me, especially pearls — which are all twinsets and class — but these were beautiful. They were large, asymmetric, colourful. I put them on — and felt them heavy and cool, lying along my neck, reaching below my collar bone.

'Where did these come from?'

My mother explained, her eyes fixed on her reflection, making up, she spoke out of the side of her mouth, glancing, as I stood admiring my neck in the mirror on the other wall. Like in the movies, we conversed in that sidelong manner, the voice of the woman putting on mascara, concentrating.

'Your grandmother gave them to me, as a third string to *add* to the double one, you know, the one we all wore for everyday — and then, I don't know maybe seven years ago I broke them, and had them restrung, and they don't *fit* anymore, I haven't worn them since, I wouldn't wear them alone. Though they look nice as a single string on you, an odd length — of course *I* couldn't wear them like that. Why don't you keep them on, darling, wear them to dinner?'

'Really, do you think they look nice? I like them, but they're really not *me*, are they.'

'Don't be silly, they look lovely on you, wear them.'

At dinner, the husband of my mother's oldest friend said to me, 'You should always wear pearls, they bring out the whites of your eyes, you should wear pearls in your hair.' I was very pleased. I wanted the pearls.

It's hard to trace how it was that I began to want the pearls, that I began to feel it was possible to want the pearls. They were beautiful. And my mother never wore them. They'd been given to her by my father's mother, her great enemy, a woman I rather liked, and took after, they said. I wanted my mother, who has nothing, to give me something, a treasure. I wanted the implication of femininity, a kind of womanliness, they seemed to hold. I wanted my mother to bestow this upon me, to give me her blessing, so to speak. For ages I'd made myself the short haired scruffy joke, a boyish mess, refusing any attempt to please. In reaction to that demonstration, depressed, I'd erased myself almost entirely, going in for invisible, practical clothes, the non-look. Then some shift had taken place, a haircut, love, I wanted to be feminine — sexy and elegant, I started to use face cream, to revive fashion, seriously exploring the possibilities of makeup, the whole routine.

Recently my mother had finally given up the pursuit of glamour, that kind of power. Did this abdication allow my taking up the feminine position? My mother clearly hadn't enjoyed her daughters encroaching on her territory, we were rivals and she did her best to disarm us, blighting our narcissism, insisting on the miseries of her life, while at the same time denying the possibility of other pursuits, different spoils. Excluding myself from female talk of sex and food, awkward, loveless, my refusal of glamour was a way to avoid this guilty struggle, as well as a failed attempt to turn the tables, refute these definitions. The struggle had finally become out of date, my mother had (sort of) given up, and for me, the gift of the pearls represented a possible gesture of forgiveness, that she was pleased to see me pretty, aiding and abetting my adventures, no longer fighting. Possibly I wanted them simply to please her.

Towards the end of the weekend, we discussed the possibility of me having the pearls. It became clear almost immediately, that while she really wanted me to have them, my mother couldn't bear to give them away. She couldn't part with them. She wanted me to have them. I didn't push it.

'No, no Mommy, I wouldn't dream of taking them from you, it's O.K., it's really all right.'

I returned to the city.

Some weeks later we arranged to meet in Boston, where we would both visit my grandmother, my mother's mother, making this visit more bearable by each other's presence. When I arrived, my mother took me upstairs, and immediately began talking about pearls. Another femininity in the bedroom scene, this time with a conspiratorial air, scheming. My mother lay flat on the bed, her favourite position for conversation, as I unpacked some things, looked out of the window, and watched my face in the mirror.

'I've figured out the pearls problem. You want *my* pearls, Grandma's pearls, right? Well Momma has some *lovely* pearls, that are actually very valuable, a double row of seed pearls, perfectly matched, I've *always* wanted them — so I've been talking to her, and I've persuaded her to give them to you. So she's going to give you those, and then we can do a swop — I'll take hers, and you can have mine, it's O.K., she's so blind she'll never know the difference.'

I was slightly horrified. Also amused: to get these pearls off my mother, she would have to be given the pearls *her* mother wouldn't part with. So that the gap where pearls once were, the vacant place in the jewel box, would be filled, by an equally unwearable, but altogether more satisfactory set of pearls.

I sidestepped the question of deceiving my grandmother by thinking, it's her mother, not mine. I was the childish accomplice. But I had to play quite an active role in this scene, the grateful recipient. As soon as we three sat down together, my mother said, her voice pitched high, 'Shall I go get your pearls, Momma, to give to Tracy?' 'Yes darling', my grandmother said, as my mother left the room. This was my cue; I managed to improvise a believable combination of pleasure and surprise, and shortly thereafter the pearls were placed in my hands, and the subject was dropped.

Later that evening I examined them. They were not beautiful. I didn't want them. They were narrow, tight, small, perfectly white, even, while mine were bulbous and yellowing, excessive. But they were worth a lot of money: for one brief shining moment I held them in my hot sticky hand, and considered the possibility of a doublecross, of giving up the pearls I wanted, and taking the money, instead. Temptation: what do you really want? Leaving aside the question of my mother's rage, I found that I really didn't want these pearls, the money, I really wanted the others, my pearls. And so the transaction was completed.

My mother and I left Momma's house, each in possession of her mother's pearls, pleased. Later, I was told that my pearls were probably very valuable indeed. I refrained from having them properly valued — I wouldn't be able to wear them any more if they were worth thousands, and that's why I wanted them, that was my pleasure, to feel them heavy on my neck, my grandmother's, my mother's pearls.

SWINE

My stepfather's golden pencil was a present from his mistress. He and my mother both thought of her as his mistress. But she was indiscreet with intent; she gave him a gold mechanical pencil and he used it constantly. Since they had been married for a relatively short time, such a serious affair, in a small town, with a woman who lived down the road, was something of a shock to my mother. The woman was a dear friend of my mother's dear friend, so it was really quite messy. They all lived in nice detached houses with gardens, within spitting distance of each other.

Every day when he came home from the office, my stepfather would empty his pockets, putting a pile of change, his keys, and his gold pencil neatly on top of his chest of drawers. In the morning, he would slide it into his inside jacket pocket, and depart for work, kissing my mother goodbye, as she stood in the kitchen in her dressing gown. Occasionally he would stop seeing his woman friend, or promise to stop seeing her. Occasionally my mother would threaten divorce, or talk to a lawyer. This state of affairs continued for years.

At one point, when they had been getting on rather better — when it seemed clear that indeed for the time being he wasn't seeing the other woman, one evening, quite late, my mother suddenly fixed on the gold pencil. As she said later, she was just *tired* of having to see this thing every day, year after year, she just didn't *need* this. Spontaneously, without hesitation, she went into the bedroom (my stepfather in the sitting room, dozing in front of the TV), found the pencil, and walked out into the garden. It was cold. There was a big lawn, and flower beds and shrubs around the place. She walked out, taking clear steps, in no specific direction, the night sky wide open, and then crouched, plunging the gold pencil point first into the ground. She buried it like a knife into flesh, vertical. It was invisible. She quickly turned and walked back into the house.

A couple of months later her dear friend told her that the other woman had cancer and had to have her eye removed. My mother's oldest friend, a dabbler in the occult, said, I always knew you were a witch. They were quite sure she'd blinded her rival by this unintended spell. Years later, for some reason, affection, wanting to share the joke, the secret, my mother confessed. (She left out the eye of course.) His only comment was, I always wondered what you'd done with it. He insisted they dig it up, a valuable object, gold. My mother tried, wandering around the garden poking the ground with a fork, but she couldn't find it again.

REPETITION

Tracy was always after the man she couldn't have; for two years she found out the pleasures of rejection, madly in love with a series of unsuitable men. Unsuitable primarily because they didn't want her; plus she made it impossible, filling up the space between her and the object with untold quantities of undying love, there was no room to manoeuvre, back against the wall, the object fled as fast as possible. She remained, heartbroken. Then, very suddenly, she would lose interest, laugh at it, until another one would hove into view, and she'd be off again. They were all maniacs, except Robert, who was just very straight; she scared the shit out of all of them.

But rejection, however passionately pursued, had nothing on triangulation, and when at last she found a man who wanted her, it was the other woman that clinched it. This time she really fell.

ADULTERY

Sleep

In thick darkness, my edges blurred with sleep, in the middle of the night, you took my hand and I touched you, feeling the space between us filled with darkness. You lay on your back, waiting, and I clambered over you, clumsy, slow, biting you gently, pushing wet against you, kissing your mouth, all sensations diffuse and intense in this darkness, sleepy. Touch, unconscious, unnamed, opposite to vision, that unavoidable interpretation activity, naming — the sense of touch makes sense differently. It is invisible, unspoken, in darkness, it fills my body with shades of more and less specific sensations, pleasure engulfs me, shadowy, I lose all sense of naming, definition, I move against you, your pale skin, naked on this bed. I feel my body expanding, limitless, the line is rubbed out, smudged, and I am part air, darkness, heat, you, pleasure. You lie under me, breathing, fucking me, deep inside, and we both feel the shock when my coming crashes over us like a wave, night crashing down, immeasurable. We lie stranded, stilled, unnamed, the night tangible, soft cover over us, darkness thick and cloudy. Muttering bits of words, lying in your arms, I go back to sleep.

Io

Alone, she was naked, smooth white skin, and he became a cloud, secretly, in order to make love to her. He embraced her, and she almost disappeared, feeling his touch everywhere. She felt the soles of her feet, the back of her neck, her stomach, her long thighs, touched, completely. When he pushed against her, she gasped with shock, this was beyond possibility, dreamy. She felt solid, her skin a surface, full and heavy, and as he sought out her recesses, brushed against her breasts, curled under her arm and around her ear, she succumbed to darkness, she lost her clear lines, round volumes of milky skin, her body began to blur, to melt with pleasure. He was huge, measureless, billowing, he moved against her, hazy, smudging her edges, until she was lost, darkness tangible invading her, the heavy darkness of her inner world, wet and mysterious body, inside, touched by this cloud of sensation, her outer definition dissolved, she was lost, cloudy.

When his wife found out, he changed Io into a white heifer, solid and smooth. A continuation: round and white and small, still, she loved to lose herself, expanding, she would merge with cloudy darkness, suffused with shadowy pleasure, she loved it. When he couldn't come to her, she stood in a field, practicing being beautiful, taking elegant heifer steps, white

136

against the trees. Her body would bring her lover again, a cool seduction in which her precision, her solid form would invite his cloudy presence, and she would again undergo transformations, blurring definition, erased, losing herself in this love.

His wife asked for the heifer as a gift, a lovely thing. He couldn't refuse. But when the guard appeared in the field, sleepless, the man who could sleep and watch at the same time, her lover was thwarted. Her white legs stepped perfectly through short grass, her head turning, the elegance of a knowing animal. She moved to please him, knowing she was watched. The guard was unmoved, utterly without interest. He didn't watch her, he watched out. She continued to take precise steps, thinking of her invisible love, absent presence, seducing him. At length he instructed his servant to kill the guard, and silvery, the messenger sent the man with a hundred eyes to sleep, playing silvery music, as she stood watching, he cut his throat. Her lover came again, and she dissolved once more. The wife's revenge was perfect, niggling, endless, a cloud of tiny flies, swarming, chasing her, and she travelled the world to escape it, engulfed in a cloud of torment, on the run, longing for that darkness, that loss.

CELIA

That night I had all my armour on, my hair made a shiny helmet, slicked down like feathers, my clothes stunned, my red lips struck blows, glancing, I even had cohorts, my elegant friends, such a comfort. That night I was determined, I wasn't going to let emotion slide me down gullies, I wasn't going to get drunk and slur into intimacy, enact ambivalence, touch. Inside your house, a big room full of your friends, my outlines were drawn clearly, I stood out like a lighthouse, intact.

Later, when you came to tell me that you'd demolished your husband, so to speak, and now I could go pick up the pieces — when you came to send me to him, I refused, I almost managed to refuse to speak. Eventually politeness overcame my wish to remain outside your play, to sidestep my lines in this your scenario, the wife addresses the girlfriend, together they murmur a cozy concern, mingling tears, we both care about him so much. When you said, 'And he hasn't eaten!', I felt this was moving into high comedy, the wife appeals to the girlfriend as good mother. I ended up feeding him scrambled eggs at two in the morning, just as you expected. But I refused to sense your expectations determining my actions, I couldn't bear to suspect I was merely following instructions, so to speak. That you'd handed him over to me, for the time being. I had my armour on, I wasn't going to be hurt, and everything you (and he) did that evening was water off a duck's back, however fast my heart was pounding.

Now I am more willing to allow your acknowledged intentions, that you were well-meaning, coming up to me in that restaurant. I almost want to explain, to make this mark disappear, explain it away, tell you why I won't collude in gestures of intimacy with you, insist that I never meant to humiliate you, I was simply completely determined not to humiliate myself. My silence made you ridiculous; your intervention made my position absurd, institutionalized within the history of your marriage, the girlfriend position. And it's impersonal, this enmity, it's structural; I never disliked you, I just would prefer it if this predicament didn't exist. Which is not to say that I would prefer it if you didn't exist — quite. We are enemies, no less. That's why I won't speak to you.

He asked me for the same again, scrambled eggs twice. Between rounds, he told me it was all over, the end of the road. The end of his relationship with you. I said, 'Nonsense!', or words to that effect. No one intended cruelty, it's simply what we worked together that evening to produce.

My familiar — I know your face so well now that when I lie down alone, resting a little in the late afternoon, knowing I'll be seeing you later, I can picture you, your face hovers over mine, pale, beautiful, ghostly. I have begun to imitate the way you stand, contraposto, and my friend Fran notes that we both say 'oh, o.k.' with exactly the same intonation. She won't venture to guess which of us initiated this practice. We both hurt our backs, fucking for hours on the floor — you'd been out of town for a couple of days, Milwaukee, you'd come back. Weeks later, back pain continues to shift between the two of us, floating, it moves from you to me, and back again. Then your ear got blocked, like mine, and I made a joke, I would ask you, how is my ear?

When we make love, the switch of masculine/feminine signifiers is speedy, intricate, overwhelming. Your passivity, my attack — manipulating pleasure to make up a sweet confusion, dodgy, hysterical, a jumping of the tracks.

I tell you all the secrets, even mine. This is what's known as a boundary problem. You expect me to know things I don't. When I am in trouble, I imagine you've figured it out already. Eventually you find me out, passive you wait, gradually it seeps out of me like black swamp water, mire, slowly becoming clearer.

After six months, we found one thing to disagree about, though I still think you fail to understand why I like Lawrence. I prefer my orange juice watered down, you like it straight from the carton. We scrutinize these marks of difference like perplexed monkeys, trying to understand what happened. But most of the time we succeed in seeming to be too alike.

When love is about narcissistic identification, then you can do no wrong. We sustain this exchange by avoiding disagreement, suppressing displeasure, and continually choosing identity.

When I see you after a separation of a day or two, it is like a part of my body was missing, I feel like an amputee, your presence restores this loss. It's all a bit too platonic for my liking, as if there were a fantasy of ideal androgyny somewhere, but you bring it back to Freud, laughing, you say, *which* part?

LOVE

If love is about primary attachment, maternal, then it is made up of a series of loss and discovery, possession and abandon. It is made out of the possibility of pain.

Tears come, seeing clearly how much I want you, and how I can't have you, and how much you are not what I want — three different pains.

Nonsense: that time when I said, in an excess of passionate attachment, I said, 'I want to marry you, but I don't get married.' You were interested in the modal logic of the sentence: 'I don't get married.' Later you said, 'You don't get married and I'm married already, that's what's called a double whammy.'

We cherish our confusion, it prolongs this absurd situation. Your coming and going make up my passion; a terrible equation in which you are the only solace for the pain you give me. It's ridiculous, intolerable.

I had a dream, a nightmare: someone died, my father, the waves came up over the cliff, and I was swept out to sea, completely, finally lost. This woke me up. When my terror subsided, tide going out, I found myself thinking of Celia, thinking of my mother, wondering how she was, where.

If love is about primary attachment, maternal, then it is made up of a series of loss and discovery, possession and abandon. It is pleasure made out of the possibility of pain.

INVISIBLE

As Tracy got out of bed, thinking of Celia, she remembered climbing into it the night before, she remembered thinking of Celia, climbing into that bed, as she thought of her waking up in it, getting up. It was as if there was some kind of terrible echo, resonating, a ghastly repetition, or imitation. She briefly felt herself to be Celia's shadow, malevolent. It was the same bed, David's bed, they were both, separately, climbing into, out of. These thoughts were very unpleasant. She was irritated that David hadn't changed the sheets. He had neither changed them before Celia's visit, nor after. So Celia got to sleep in her, Tracy's, dirty sheets, and Tracy got Celia's. She decided not to think; she decided not to think, about Celia, or David. At the same moment she decided to wash the sheets. She shouted, 'I'm going to wash your sheets I don't care how ideologically unsound it is,' as David vanished into his bath, and she started to pull the bright red sheets off the bed. Tracy hadn't set foot in this flat since Celia's visit, she'd slept with David at her place every night. The slightest change was a sign of Celia, a mark of her presence. Tracy felt very anxious, when the sheets were on the floor. She headed for the kitchen, thinking, there's a difference between David's oven, and mine — it takes longer, I should put the broiler on now. Tracy and David ate the same breakfast every morning; every morning she toasted the english muffins in the broiler at the bottom of the stove, made the tea, so it would be ready when he came out of the bath. She put the kettle on, and turned on the oven, opening the fridge door. She checked to see the gas had lit itself under the kettle. The fridge produced more imaginary repetitions, more signs of Celia. Lots of things were rotten; Tracy stood by the open door of the fridge, dropping things into the garbage bag under the sink. She threw out a quarter of soggy melon, thinking, Celia's melon. She poured sour milk down the drain. Looking at the kitchen counter, she saw Lipton's tea. Bought by Celia, she thought. She must have drunk a lot of tea when she was here. Shutting the door of the fridge, Tracy declared silent and clear, stop thinking this. Stop.

She walked back into the big room. David was in his bath. She stood in the middle of the room, not thinking. After a while she smelled gas. Of course, she thought, that's the difference, you have to *light* this oven. She went back to the stove, opened the oven door, and lit a match. There was a very loud bang and she was enveloped in a pillar of flame. The first scream. She sensed crackling heat: her hair on fire. She put her hands to her head, screaming again. At this point David appeared, wet and naked, Tracy remembered nothing of this, how she moved into the bathroom, to throw water on her skin, wet her hair. She stood by the sink, in front of the mirror, in shock, trying to be ordinary. She said, 'Don't let me interrupt your bath, get back into your bath.' Her shirt was covered in black dust, as if after a volcano. The smell of burned hair was heavy in the air, a sense of sour smoke and cold water: she kept splashing cold water over her face and arms. Her skin hurt like sunburn. There was no hair at all on her right forearm. The hair on her upper lip had shrivelled and darkened without burning off entirely. Her eyebrows and eyelashes were only slightly burned. Her hair was a disaster: falling forward, it had protected her face; pulling a comb through, clumps of charred hair came off. It was now many different lengths, with the scorched ends of burned hair. Her sense of relief, not dead yet, shifted into a sense of how much damage had been done; Tracy suddenly became very upset. She was scared he would think her vain, crying over her hair. She walked out of the bathroom, and couldn't find a private place, in this one big room. Remembering the balcony, she opened the door, and stood in the part where you couldn't be seen from inside, facing out, she sobbed and choked and shuddered, with horror, exposed to the world. She saw no one looking at her, but the block of flats opposite had a hundred identical balconies, making some kind of audience. It was cold, white light from à grey sky, morning. She felt like an aberration, with her wet, charred hair and her sore skin, she felt very very ugly.

'Oh *there* you are,' he said, finding her. They embraced, wetly, and she came back inside, to recline on the bed for a minute, while he made the breakfast. 'It must be the adultery,' she said. He described lying in the bath, he said the bang was very dramatic, and the two screams.

'I knew exactly what had happened immediately, I had this image of you, like in a dream, lying on the floor with flames all along your body, going up, woman in flames, and I jumped out of the bath, to save you — though clearly I wasn't thinking very hard because I didn't grab the towels . . .'

That was when Tracy found out she couldn't remember David coming into the kitchen, or how she got into the bathroom. He told her that he had done the same thing, when he first moved in, not so extremely, he'd singed his eyebrows; he told her he'd wasted an inordinate amount of time accusing himself of stupidity, that she mustn't do that.

'Yes but I *knew* it was a stupid thing to do, I was so calm, I remember lighting the match, I *knew*, I must have known. Such a suicidal gesture. Self-immolation? Adultery.'

'It sounds like a sin, the way you say it.'

They spoke of adultery, veering off onto the differences between the seven deadly sins and the ten commandments. Different orders of responsibility, how the woman always gets punished, stoned to death and so on; somewhere in here she got confused and gave up.

'I must be trying to make myself ugly, to ruin my looks, since you take such pleasure in them. I want to make myself a monster.'

'You look *great*, you look amazing now, I know it's a ridiculous thing to say, but you do, you look beautiful, it's because —'

'What, like I'm all there?'

'*Yes*, like you're really interested in everything, really excited.'

'Yes, that's how I feel.'

They drank tea. He asked if the milk was all right.

'I'm not sure it's the milk, it might be this *tea*.'

'Oh this *tea*, ugh, Lipton's.'

Tracy walked into the bathroom for more cold splashing, she heard him call after her: 'Well *I* didn't buy it.' Slightly shocked at his levity, she made a play, a drama, to push his joke further, make it better.

'*What*! *That's* worse than the tea, you're asking me to drink tea *she* bought?' They laughed hard at this, in different rooms.

Later David said, 'It was so odd, I didn't know where you'd gone, I couldn't find you. I thought the lump of pillows on the bed might be you, or of course you might have left, but I couldn't believe that, and your bag was still here, your coat, so I thought you might be in the closet, hiding,' — Tracy laughed. 'Maybe someone in shock would hide in a cupboard, childhood and all that, and then finally I remembered there was another door, because I thought I'd heard a door handle turn, I remembered the balcony, and found you.'

'Yes I was embarrassed to cry in front of you, but I knew I had to, to loosen the shock, there was nowhere else to go.'

They met again in the evening, and went out to dinner,

Japanese. He talked about the lecture he'd given that afternoon, Walter Benjamin, she listened, laughing. Eating sushi, they sat side by side, turning towards, away from each other.

'So what did *you* do today?'

'The only serious thinking I did was to try to figure out why I set myself on fire this morning.'

'Tell me.'

'I'm a bit reluctant to go into it — I don't know.' She paused. 'It was the sheets. Thinking about it, I understood that it was an act to obliterate Celia, washing the sheets would be both eliminating the physical traces of her body, and at the same time taking her place, somehow, the wife. It seemed like such an aggressive, such a presumptuous thing to do —'

'But I *don't* understand, why do you have to blow yourself up?'

'It's not guilt exactly, more like necessity.'

'I don't see it.'

'You don't know — I didn't talk about it, every moment I was in your flat I was doing this double thing of thinking and not-thinking about Celia, like very attentive to any sign of her presence and at the same time the most rigorous suppression. The bed, the tea she bought, the food in the fridge — Celia's melon, I thought, as I dropped it into the garbage — which is ironic actually because today I realised it was *my* melon in fact, I left it there in your fridge, whenever it was, when I came round to watch the Academy Awards —'

'You said you knew there was a difference between your cooker and mine, what's this difference?'

'Difference. There is a very important difference between us — Celia. You cross over, into the world that not only excludes me, but pretends I don't *exist*. I *can't* cross over, I'm obliterated, invisibled out.'

'And what did you actually see in the kitchen, what did you notice?'

'I told you, her tea, the rotten food I imagined belonged to

145

her. But everything spoke of her — you remember last night, when I arrived, you remember when I tried to open the window —'

'*That* was spectacular. I couldn't believe you didn't hurt yourself.'

'No it was like slapstick, trying to catch the books, slippery — I just fell flat on my face. Thwack. It was comic. But you know what I was *thinking*, I was thinking this window's impossible to open, *I* got this window open three months ago, it's stayed open ever since, only Celia could have closed it, what a *stupid* thing to do — whereupon I fall flat on my face.'

'Yes it was pretty stunning. And it was odd because you so *nearly* caught the books, stopped them falling, it was so nearly a perfect action.'

'Um I don't know, I think it was doomed from the start.'

'So, this morning, do you remember which matches you used?'

'My own, I think, I found my matches. I don't remember.'

'You don't remember seeing any matches?'

'Nope — what, in the kitchen? No — I don't think so. Why?'

'Well, as far as I am aware there are only two things in the flat that Celia left, two things she bought while she was here — the tea, and there were some matches.'

Tracy laughed and laughed and laughed. 'I don't believe it, it's too perfect, she left me matches to blow myself up with?'

'It does seem extraordinary to me that you don't remember seeing the matches, there's a pack of Camels and boxes of matches in the kitchen, in plain sight.'

'She smokes Camels? What, filtered or plain, unfiltered?'

'I'm not sure, unfiltered.'

'I always used to smoke plain Camels.'

'You see it was a *sequence* of bungled actions — when I turned the oven off I saw that you hadn't turned the knob all the way to Broil —'

'*Hadn't* I?'

'No. Which is one reason why your explosion was so much

worse than mine — the oven itself was full of gas. *Then* you wandered off, without lighting it, *then* you smelled gas (from the other room, no less), and *lit* it. *Three* bungled actions, it was a *series* of bungled actions.'

'Yes, obviously I really *wanted* to blow myself up. I'm just knocked out that she left me those matches — we *are* psychic warriors — you don't know. Months ago, I had a dream, I came across it the other day, I dreamed that I was at a party at your house, this was long before your party, and Celia had black hennaed hair, snaky and thick, and white painted face, lots of eye makeup, like an egyptian, or medusa, and in this dream she launched into this tirade, that was really — awful, she was incredibly powerful, and I just thought, get me out of here, but I said, to distract her, to take revenge, I said — Your hair is really beautiful, can I touch it. Like pulling the carpet out from under her, by holding up a mirror, by referring to her appearance. And of course that's so close to what really happened, when you gave that party —'

'Yes, *hair*, now it begins to make sense —'

'When she came out with her immortal line — David told me how *depressed* you've been all week because of your new *haircut*, but I think it looks very well, in fact I told David at the time that I didn't *remember* what your hair was like, but you know, now I will, it's really very striking —'

'O.K. O.K.'

'And the student who mistook me for her, last week, he kept going on about her hair and my hair — she's *shorter* than you, he kept saying, and her hair is shorter —'

'Which isn't true.'

'I don't remember. She's out of sight, I don't *see* her, ever, I only have an *idea* of her — made out of some dreams, wishing, fear, guilt — that's oedipal, adulterous — with a little corner of memory to build the whole elaborate fantasy on. She stands in for my own imaginary self-accusation, and obviously it's impossible for me to judge the overlap between this picture of righteous injury and what Celia might really be about. I'm

147

the other woman, invisible, I make her into the wicked witch of the west, evil queen, sphinx, medusa — I have a suspicion that I *need* to picture her vengeful, cruel, I construct her in fantasy as a punitive audience to this illicit love affair, Mommy — I think it may even be a crucial element in the invention of this passion, my love for you, the key ingredient that adds such a poignant edge to our pleasures —'

'Don't —'

'I *wanted* short hair, I burn my hair off, to have short hair, to be your boy — *she* can be the woman, I won't challenge her position. I will have short hair, I won't have babies, I will be a boy, your bit on the side.'

'Babies?'

'Yes yes obviously, *she's* the woman with books and babies, remember? And I've got none.'

'But we'd just been talking about that — the night before. About having babies —'

'Oven, bun in the oven — I make it blow up in my face. If I do not speak my distress, eventually it will blow up in my face. You see, darling, I wanted you to *say* it — you asked me if *I* wanted kids ever, and I told you what I think about all that, and I said, why?, and you said, just inquiring. I wanted you to say — oh that in the real world you most probably don't want any more kids, but in fantasy you would like to have children with me, sometime.'

'Of course I think about it, I'm so in love with you — darling let's go, I'm exhausted, I am *so tired.*'

'Yes, so am I.'

In bed, beginning to make love, he very gently started to slap her face. 'I don't know how to play,' she said, 'this is serious.' He offered his face, ironical; she made a fist and socked him, hard, in the side of his mouth, as men do in westerns. He was surprised, he said he was scared his teeth were going to fall out. They made love, fighting with each other. At one point she found his hand in hers, his left hand, and she twisted it, hard, saying — 'And I *don't* like this fucking *wedding* ring . . .' This infuriated him; it was a real fight now. After, he said he thought what she'd said about the ring was completely gratuitous, he repeated this word over and over; he'd always worn rings, he wore lots of different rings, was he supposed to avoid certain fingers — ? Tracy said, 'No no I have no wish for you to change your practice I only said it to hurt you. You see how dangerous it is playing out violence with me, I don't know how to pretend. I only said it to hurt you.'

They lay together in bed, holding on to each other, sounds of a fight in the street came in. He lifted his head. A man and a woman shouting. Quietly, he said, 'What do you think's going on out there?'

'Another tragedy.'

'Another. Another what?'

'Another tragedy, another New York tragedy.'

At this point he withdrew completely. She pursued him.

'You really do disappear don't you.'

'I just feel terribly depressed.'

'Why.'

'You've been pushing all night — your insistence, your insistence on tragedy is so fucking relentless . . .'

'You're just beginning to see how destructive I can be. Or whatever the word is — I don't like that word, destructive. Violent.'

'I just think it's got to stop, enough, you know? Celia left over a week ago, the aftermath has gone on just a little too long.'

'Yes, you're right.'

'It can't go on.'

'I know. But look what you won't acknowledge is the *difference* in our positions, how hard this is for me. I mean, if *I* get a re-run of the oedipal situation, daddy and mummy, and all the guilt and ambivalence and complex identifications that entails, what *you* get is two mummies — a good mummy and a bad mummy, separate, interchangeable — what more could any man want?'

'Yes but it's more complicated than that.'

'Of course, but on some level that's what's going on — it's structural. What seems to be happening, what seems to be the case, is — that *my* fantasy relation to Celia threatens our relationship *more* than your real relation. Possibly. That's what I'm trying to show you.'

'Maybe. I don't know.'

'Shall we go to sleep now.'

'Yes darling. I love you.'

'I love you.'

In the morning they'd both been dreaming. She climbed over him, pale, entirely passive, beginning to kiss his neck.

'Do you want me to fuck you.'

'I'm feeling a bit fragile, I think — not now, not right now.'

'O.K. That's O.K.'

'I'm still *tired* —'

'I'm not surprised, after what I put you through last night —'

She felt too big, lying on top of him, too much. They separated. A little later he touched her, and they began to make love, no pain. They got up then, leaving marks of come on the sheet. He had his bath while she did breakfast. There was a glimmer of terror when she turned the oven on. She picked up two glasses from beside the bed, and putting them in the sink, Tracy dropped the one full of water. It poured over her thighs, and fell, breaking into a million pieces.

'*Shit*.'

'Tracy?'

She raised her voice: 'It's O.K., it's O.K., I just broke a glass, it was full of water so there's a mess —'

David appeared, naked and wet, laughing, he stood looking at her stranded, surrounded by broken glass.

'*Another* bungled action, I'm so pleased — this is great. It's not just *my* kitchen. Maybe we can have a bungled action at every breakfast —'

'No I don't think so.'

'We've had fire, and water — let's see — air, air could be a bit nasty.'

'What like choking to death? Or throwing myself off your balcony?'

'Catching your finger in a fan —'

'Maybe we should start scripting them, to keep them under control. I suppose falling down the other night was earth.'

'*Yes*, yes.'

'Get back into your bath.'

Tracy was determined to avoid cutting herself on the glass; she picked bits up with extreme care, her brain whizzing as she attempted associations, followed her action through to some kind of meaning. David reappeared and she let him have it.

'I've made up a theory about why I'm pouring water all over myself this morning, as opposed to setting myself on fire yesterday . . . It's that I was lying in bed, this morning, just now, puddles of come, and I was thinking, come, it's so funny, how odd it is — sperm swimming around like crazy — and every time you *come* you — make this mess — so to speak — (whereas when *I* come there's no sign, other than my pleasure, it's invisible?) — anyway, and then I make this mess on myself and break a glass — so I think's it's about *impregnation* darling. I'm trying to get pregnant.'

'Yes — that would confirm the oven —'

'Yup, I knew you would like this, because it supports the oven diagnosis, the *oven* hypothesis. Femininity. It's very classical, isn't it, the young girl spills water on herself, breaks a glass. I feel like I'm acting out dreaming. Slightly mad. At least I didn't cut my finger, I didn't *prick* my finger on a piece of glass . . .'

'Yes that would have been too much, just a little over the top — Sleeping Beauty all over again . . .'

'Oh no, not that.'

On the way out to dinner, in the elevator, they kissed, leaning against the wall, and she heard a shift, a movement.

'Look, we can make the elevator move,' she cried, impulsive, and flung herself gently against him, pushing him against the wall. The elevator shuddered. She continued to knock her body, his body, against it, throwing herself around the elevator, thrilled by ever more frightening sounds. He was laughing, nervous, a high sharp laugh; she thought he was kidding when he said he was scared, asked her to stop. She jumped up and down as hard as she could, banging against the wall, him, slaphappy, pleased, amused by the effects she was producing.

Later, after dinner, in bed, David said, 'I was frightened in the elevator.'

'Really, really, were you? How completely extraordinary. *I* wasn't. What, did you think it would fall, break?'

'No, I was — it was more that I was frightened of you.'

'How do you mean?'

'I just thought, it showed what you were capable of. Someone who is capable of this could do more extreme things in different circumstances . . .'

'Like what?'

'I don't know, like drive a car into a tree . . .'

'Oh yes, too too Iris Storm. No I wasn't frightened at all, I didn't care. I mean, I didn't believe the elevator could break, would break, but you know what it's like when you feel completely reckless, I didn't *care*, I didn't care whether it broke or not.'

Tracy was silent for a moment. Then she said, 'It's because I want to kill you.'

'Do you?', he said, politely, as he turned over to go to sleep.

The next morning, after he left, Tracy sat at her table, scribbling. When she looked up, all she could see was the grime on the windows, emphatic in the bright sun. She decided to wash them. She saw herself perched on the ledge, clutching her bottle of windex and her roll of paper towels, one leg uncomfortably shoved inside, ballast, the other kneeling under her, as she reached, toppled, and fell, into the street, six floors below — a sudden death. She decided not to. Then she made herself do it, without falling. After, the windows were so clean, so clear in the sunlight, they were invisible.